CHAPTER ONE

'So you have come as a peace-maker to reunite the bitterly divided clans of Ransan and Bonnet?'

'Yes,' answered Isabelle Bonnet simply. She detected but did not resent the very gentle mockery in the rich and rather throaty voice of the elderly woman who sat opposite her, pouring coffee and setting out warm croissants.

'Ah! You have the optimism of the young,' Claire Oudot said. It was a delighted crow in French, which was the mother tongue of both of them. 'You will do me the world of good!'

'You don't look to me as if you're much in need of that sort of tonic, Madame Oudot,' Isabelle pointed out cheerfully.

Beneath its bright make-up, seventy-year-old Madame Oudot's face looked its age and her beautifully coiffed hair was suitably grey. It was such a very lustrous, silvery grey, however, that many a blonde might have envied it, and the wicked, gossip-loving curiosity and zest for living reflected in Madame Oudot's expression gave her rouge-covered wrinkles an extremely attractive mobility.

'Well, one must not complain,' she said, 'or walk about like a sack of old potatoes with the face of a tombstone, no matter what aches and pains one feels inside.'

Having met her for the first time just half an hour ago, Isabelle had loved her on sight, which was fortunate as Isabelle would be living in the tiny apartment above this much grander one for the indefinite future. She took in the elegant, high-ceilinged salon and it really dawned on her for the first time that this was France, and she was here.

The exultant realisation seemed to propel her to her feet with its own power, and she was too impatient for coffee and croissants just yet. She simply had to look out of the window! Wouldn't there be a perfect view of the River Loque? There was. It looped like a Greek omega to enclose the old city of Vesanceau, and on this quiet autumn Sunday morning created tranquil, green-tinted reflections of the stately stone façades belonging to the tall houses that overlooked the water.

Madame Oudot watched her energy and enthusiasm appreciatively. 'You are not tired after your flight?'

'Not in the slightest,' Isabelle answered. 'I should be, I guess...'

'How many hours was it?'

'Oh, I can't even work it out. L-o-ong!'

'And when do you start at the hospital?'

'Tomorrow, although I expect the first few days will be orientation.'

'Tomorrow!'

'I like to get my teeth into things.' Isabelle gave a wide smile, revealing said teeth—very white and even—which again had Madame Oudot clucking in admiration.

'You are very much like your mother,' the French woman declared with a degree of emotion. 'Now, please sit down and tell me her news. Does she know of your mission of diplomacy, for example?'

'My... Oh, this ridiculous enmity between *Papa* and his cousin?'

'You are so sure that it is ridiculous?' came the gentle query.

'Well, not to have spoken for thirty-five years just because *Maman* broke her engagement to François Ransan in order to go to Canada with my father! After all, Cousin

"Do you know the scenarios I had today about what was wrong?" Jacques asked.

"You'll laugh if I tell you…so I will, because I know you like to laugh and I love to hear it. Isabelle's married, I thought. She has a husband in British Columbia. Maybe two husbands! And she's lied about her age."

"Oh, Jacques! Nothing nearly so terrible as that! There's no real drama or scandal…."

LILIAN DARCY currently lives in Australia's capital with her historian husband and their growing family. They also spend significant amounts of time in the United States. Lilian has written over forty medically based romances for Harlequin, and also writes for Silhouette.

Lilian enjoys travel, quilting, gardening and reading, and is a volunteer with Australia's State Emergency Service. Readers can write to her at P.O. Box 381, Hackensack, NJ 07602, or e-mail to lildarcy@austarmetro.com.au.

Lilian Darcy

INCURABLY ISABELLE

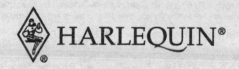

HARLEQUIN®

TORONTO • NEW YORK • LONDON
AMSTERDAM • PARIS • SYDNEY • HAMBURG
STOCKHOLM • ATHENS • TOKYO • MILAN • MADRID
PRAGUE • WARSAW • BUDAPEST • AUCKLAND

ISBN 0-373-18814-5

INCURABLY ISABELLE

First North American Publication 2003.

François did marry, too, didn't he, and rather soon afterwards? He didn't exactly die of a broken heart!'

'Ah, so that is what you have been told…' Following her own train of thought, Isabelle almost didn't catch the softly murmured exclamation.

'You mean he *did* die of a broken heart?' she demanded sharply. 'That's…!'

'No, no! Of course not. He married, as you said, and had the fine son—Dr Jacques Ransan—whom you will encounter rather soon, I think.'

'Well, I hope so! Otherwise I won't be able to be much of a peace-maker, will I? When I found out that he was a pulmonary specialist it seemed almost like an omen since I've been nursing mainly chest patients myself on a women's medical ward for nearly three years. I wonder how much *he* has been told—if he's been kept in the dark as I was until so recently. I'm sure he must find the whole thing as ridiculous as I do!'

'Do not assume too much, Isabelle,' the elderly woman cautioned. 'You are incurably impulsive, aren't you, my dear?'

'Oh, I wouldn't say that, Madame Oudot!' Isabelle protested. 'It took me almost a year to organise this job. Believe me, there was plenty of red tape to discourage a mere momentary impulse.'

'Ah, yes, but having had to wait so long,' the beautifully coiffed head cocked neatly to one side, 'what is it that you intend now? To propose peace talks during a ward round? Or make a telephone call and announce your existence, your arrival…and your intentions?'

'Something like that, I guess…only please don't put it in such terms! You're making fun of me, *madame,* and it isn't kind!'

'No, no, you are right, of course.' Beringed, stiff-jointed hands waved in the air, and the old face fell guiltily. 'It isn't kind. But, my dear...' she leaned forward, smoothing an elegant pale blue skirt '...it would not be kind, either, to let you leap into this thing with all your so-charming enthusiasm and have you discover that you had at once earned yourself an enemy by opening old wounds.'

'An enemy?' Isabelle queried sharply. 'You mean Jacques Ransan?'

'Yes, I do...'

'But, surely, after all this time, would he react that way? A member of the next generation, and an intelligent, successful man—a medical specialist, for heaven's sake...! What are you suggesting? That I make no attempt to contact him privately and at the hospital, if we meet, I say *nothing* about who I am?'

'Yes,' Madame Oudot answered gently, 'exactly that!'

'But it defeats the whole purpose of my coming here!'

'My dear, I am simply asking you to bide your time.'

'That seems...very deceitful...'

'Ah, no! Why?' Madame Oudot sat up, ramrod straight and a little indignant. 'Sensible, not deceitful! This passion for honesty is something you have picked up in British Columbia. It is, decidedly, *not* a trait of French women! We have always known how to keep the right secrets. I myself have been... But there! That is not relevant now. Please! Forget for the moment this so-American idea of honesty...'

Isabelle grinned somewhat defiantly. 'Well, I *am* American. *Canadian,* that is. You can't appropriate me completely for France. And I'm not convinced that honesty can be claimed by any country as a national trait anyway. Don't you think I should tackle this my way?'

Her way. Forthright, upbeat, fair. And, no, she didn't consider these things particularly 'American' traits.

Feminine wiles—the kinds of things that Claire Oudot was proudly expert at, it seemed—were foreign to her, and

beneath the dark, petite sparkle of her very French pretti-
ness Isabelle was still at heart the spirited and down-to-
earth tomboy she had been as a child. She did *not* like
intrigue!

But there was a flicker of alarm now in the bright old
eyes that watched her.

'Your way? No, I don't! Isabelle… Fools rush in where
angels fear to tread,' Madame Oudot enunciated in heavily
accented English, her voice wobbling slightly. 'Please, for
me, humour an old woman and bide your time. Settle in!
And accept that there may be…*complexities*…' She
squeezed her hands together convulsively, then tried to still
them in her lap.

'I've never thought of myself as either an angel or a
fool,' Isabelle answered slowly and reluctantly, watching
Madame Oudot covertly.

The poor woman really did seem upset, although she was
trying not to show it. There was a rasping note of real
urgency in her voice as she clasped her hands together
again and said, 'Please! Promise me, Isabelle! It's the only
thing I shall ask of you. Promise me that you won't tell
Jacques Ransan who you are, at least for the time being.
Trust my judgement. Wait until you see for yourself. *Promise* me!'

'All right, Madame Oudot,' Isabelle answered at last,
alarmed at the currents of emotion she saw in the small
woman and instinctively wanting to do what she could to
calm the turbulent waters. I promise, for the time being.'

'And you'll come to me when the time is right *before*
you say anything to him?'

'Yes, if you're so sure that it's important.'

'You'll see I'm right, my dear. You will!' the tiny
Frenchwoman said, her mood noticeably lighter now.

'Yes, I'm sure,' Isabelle replied dutifully. 'Tell me,

though, do you know Jacques Ransan very well?' she added after a small pause.

'Not quite as well as he knows certain parts of me, I expect. He's my doctor!'

Claire Oudot's doctor. A mere mortal in other words although, after hearing his praises sung relentlessly for a good fifteen minutes, Isabelle was left with the distinct impression that Jacques Ransan must have turned himself from stone into flesh and stepped down from a prominent position as one of the carved saints in the nearby Église Saint-Paul purely in order to brighten Vesanceau with his miraculous presence.

He was the best of all possible doctors: 'So patient and courteous with old people, who can be so impossibly difficult! And I ought to know since I am one!' The best of all possible sons: 'So loyal to his father, and such a source of pride to him!' The best of all possible men: 'Why he isn't yet married, at the age of thirty-four... It is not through the fault of the girls in this city, I can tell you!'

And handsome, too, of course, Isabelle was left to assume.

By the end of the paean of praise she might have been heartily sick of her second cousin—the man whose grandfather was her own grandmother's brother—if she hadn't been so curious about him. It was odd, though, surely, that such a paragon of masculine virtues should be so petty—if Claire Oudot was right about this—in his determination to keep alive such a very meaningless family rift after so long. Never one to slavishly take on another's opinions, Isabelle soon found herself creating her own character portrait of Dr Jacques Ransan.

Handsome, she would grant him that. Dark, undoubtedly. Smooth-featured, built like a model for expensive Italian suits, but with a shallow selfishness to him—showing perhaps in a pouting around the over-full mouth—that Claire

Oudot had not perceived because he was a shameless flatterer when he thought it would get him somewhere. Smugly arrogant, over-judgemental... Hot-tempered, too... No, *cold*-tempered, possessing a sinister, slow-simmering rage that never forgot the most trivial of insults.

Or something.

With settling into her apartment and a full schedule of orientation activities at the hospital, Isabelle had far too much to do and think about over the next week to dwell on or embellish her fanciful picture of the man, and she wasn't the type to brood or be obsessive.

It wasn't until the second week that Jacques Ransan was thrust into the forefront of her thoughts again.

Plunging into the immediate unceasing activity of a morning shift on the women's medical ward at seven a.m. on Monday, she saw his name listed alongside that of several patients, and the defiantly negative image she had formed of the man a week ago sprang back into vivid life out of the dormant place it had occupied at the back of her mind since then. Those spoiled, pouting lips, that over-glossy black hair, and his habit of fawning over the women—particularly the rich ones—under his care.

Somehow, too, she had become much more convinced that Madame Claire—'your mother's oldest friend'—was right in exacting from her that rather grim promise of secrecy. Better to wait before she told Jacques Ransan who she was. Give herself a chance to assess him, and a chance to find out a little more—because she had the strong impression that Claire knew more than she was prepared to admit about that broken engagement long ago. For now, she would focus on her work and she soon suspected that, with all there was to do on this twenty-eight-bed ward on the fourth floor, it would be difficult to do anything else.

'We're short of staff!' snapped the rather sharp-faced ward sister, Simone Boucher, at the start of the shift, glaring from behind her owlish metal-framed spectacles and pursing a mouth painted in a most unfortunate shade of orange-pink. 'No one is going into nursing these days, for reasons I can at times understand only too well!'

She glared at Isabelle, who immediately felt that perhaps she was a fool not to have been swayed by those reasons herself.

'So I hope you are capable of working with speed and efficiency?'

'I hope so, too,' Isabelle returned honestly. 'It's bound to be a bit different here, but I certainly have in the past.'

Then the sharp face softened. 'Ah! Good! Forgive me, my children are sick and I have had little sleep. In reality, things are not so bad. Now, you will be taking care of several patients today, including a new admission we are expecting this morning, and there are a number of things you should know...'

It's faintly possible I might like her after all, Isabelle was able to conclude a few minutes later.

Sister Boucher was not exaggerating about the ward's level of activity, however. The ailments they dealt with ran the gamut—respiratory, digestive, urinary, dermatological—which necessitated a multi-disciplinary approach, with visits from numerous different specialists—each with his own demands. Madame Masson's blood test, Madame Leblanc's quarter-hourly observations, Madame Truche's preventative care for bedsores.

'And Madame Seguin is to have her medicines changed,' Sister Boucher announced. 'We are awaiting the doctor to write new orders.'

It wasn't until she was well into the morning's routine that Isabelle realised that Madame Seguin was one of the patients who had 'Dr Ransan' scrawled on the card at the foot of her bed. She noticed the fact as she was skimming out of the four-bed room on her way back to the nurses'

station after doing Madame Leblanc's observations, and
when she went back ten minutes later to check on Madame
Masson before her trip across to Radiology the man himself
was there.

It came as a shock, which was silly. After all, she had
known she would meet him very soon. Perhaps that was
it—subconsciously she had allowed herself to become quite
keyed up.

And now, watching him, she was distracted from focusing on her own patient so that she started guiltily when
Madame Masson asked nervously, 'Will it hurt?'

'No, no,' she answered quickly, annoyed that she hadn't
seen for herself the fear in the seventy-two-year-old
woman's face. 'It's just a couple of X-rays, *madame,* to see
if we can find out what's causing those upsetting digestive
symptoms of yours. It won't hurt at all, and you'll be back
within an hour.'

'Well, I don't mind being wheeled about. A bit of an
outing. Oh, might I brush my hair before I go?'

'Would you like me to do it?'

'Yes, please. I do have trouble with my right arm at the
moment.'

'It won't be a professional coiffure, I'm afraid.' And fit-
ting it in would be a squeeze…

Gently brushing the neat grey waves a few moments
later, Isabelle had herself in an ideal position to see exactly
what Dr Ransan was doing with his patient in the opposite
bed.

He was as dark as she had imagined, and good-looking
in just the superficial way she had expected. She *didn't* like
his voice, though, finding it over-precise and condescend-
ing in tone as he asked Madame Seguin some careless,
perfunctory questions.

Then, just as she had finished with Madame Masson's
hair and the orderly had arrived to take her off to

Radiology, the black-haired doctor straightened, scribbled the revised drug orders on the patient's chart and summoned Isabelle with a clipped, impatient, 'Nurse?'

'Yes, Doctor,' she answered just as crisply, and she would have met his liquid black eyes quite steadily if he had deigned to look in her direction.

'She needs the bedpan. See to it, will you?'

No, she definitely didn't like his voice *or* his manner, and he still hadn't condescended to glance at her at all. She murmured a wooden acceptance of his order but was fuming inside now. Yes, I know it's my job, but need you look quite so disgusted?

She was about to brush past him to carry out his terse instruction when he *did* look at her at last, and all at once his manner changed.

'Ah!' Now that precise, clipped voice had turned very, very creamy. 'New? I'd have remembered *this* face if I'd seen it before! And I hope I'll have the chance to get to know it better.'

'Yes, well, not until I've brought Madame Seguin her bedpan,' Isabelle retorted darkly, her brown-eyed gaze still sweeping over him in an assessment that was more frank than she realised.

Yuk! she was thinking.

Her respect for Claire Oudot's judgement plummeted and her opinion of her own mother's taste in men rose proportionately. If François Ransan was anything like his sleazy son no wonder she married *Papa* instead!

The darkly handsome doctor was laughing immoderately at her line about the bedpan—which hadn't even been a joke, merely an attempt to fob him off. Now he put out his hand to shake hers.

'What exquisite skin you have!' he murmured.

Belatedly, and with lightning speed, she slid her hand from his. 'Yes... Right... Um, but Madame Seguin's bedpan…' Claire was right! I may *never* reveal my relationship to this man!

'Of course, but as I have something more…er…medically urgent for your attention I'm sure she can wait…'

He must have been *very* sure and it must have been *very* urgent because he gave neither Isabelle nor Madame Seguin herself any opportunity to protest, sweeping the former out of the room and into a tiny store-room along the corridor—following a route that was clearly far too familiar to him.

Pushing Isabelle ahead of him, he glanced along the corridor with a frown. The lift had just arrived, but before it could fully disgorge its occupants he had darted into the cupboard-sized space and closed the door behind him.

'You were showing your feelings…your interest…fully in your face, *mademoiselle*,' he crooned rapidly. 'I like that in a woman—that she is prepared to be frank about her desire.'

The sinister bud of Isabelle's suspicions flowered into a ghastly bloom of certainty as his arms closed boldly around her waist to pull her jarringly against his hips.

'Oh, for heaven's sake! You've got completely the wrong idea!' she said through clenched teeth, biting back with difficulty a stronger protest that would have burnt her professional bridges for ever with the man.

'Oh, come on, *chérie*, I saw it in your eyes from the first moment.'

'I don't see how since you didn't even look at me,' she retorted bluntly, enraged.

But he was braying with laughter at her protests, his arms—and at the moment he seemed to have about six of them—still winding around her, chafing impatiently at her new white uniform. 'What a delightfully tart tongue! We are going to make wonderful music together, you and I, Sister…er…'

He made a grab for her name badge, but Isabelle was too fast for him, clapping her own hand over it just in time to protect her breast from his groping touch.

Name badge. Now, there was a thought! She looked at his, and with an inner groan wondered why on earth she hadn't thought to check it before. DR REMY CHAPUIS. This ghastly man wasn't Jacques Ransan at all.

The door opened abruptly and Dr Chapuis's uncomfortably realistic impersonation of an octopus came to a sudden and welcome end. His jaw dropped in embarrassment and he flushed. A tall man stood there.

Tall? That was inadequate. *Very* tall. Loose-limbed, lankily posed, earnest and intellectual behind tortoiseshell-framed spectacles, and dressed in a light-coloured suit. Rather benign-looking at first glance, despite his height, yet somehow Remy Chapuis was now looking as nervous as a new private before a legendary drill sergeant, and he volunteered hastily—before he could be asked—'You were quite right. Madame Seguin's medicines do need to be changed. Mademoiselle...um...er and I were just discussing it.'

The tall man said nothing, although a brief, hoarse sound did escape his lips behind a balled hand. Isabelle felt an oddly urgent need to wrest those spectacles from his face to get a closer look at his eyes. Needless to say, she resisted it and said very firmly, 'I was looking for a bedpan, but I see this isn't where they're kept. Excuse me.'

And since dignity and brevity were the only possible ways of saving a shred of equanimity from the situation, she said nothing further and simply left, edging her way past Dr Chapuis and sliding through the narrow space between the tall man and the door. A rasp—of displeasure, perhaps—came from his throat as she did so, and she brushed against him more strongly than she had realised she would, having misjudged the gap in her haste.

But she was free now and didn't pause to look back, didn't listen to the rapid, whispered exchange taking place at the store-room door. And here were the bedpans, in this second room on the right, so poor Madame Seguin's wait would soon be over.

As for Dr Chapuis...

'Watch out for that one!' Sister Boucher told her during a snatched pause some ten minutes later. 'You're pretty, so I have no doubt he'll—' She caught sight of Isabelle's eloquent face. 'He already has? My goodness, it must be a record!'

'I resisted,' Isabelle assured her.

'Good! Fortunately, he's fairly harmless.' Sister Boucher smiled, and, with her lipstick now largely transferred to the rim of her coffee-cup, it was evident that she actually had a very pretty mouth.

Isabelle was bold enough to ask now, 'But Dr Ransan... Isn't Madame Seguin supposed to be *his* patient?'

'Yes, but it is doubtful that he will be in today. He is sick,' came the rapid, abrupt explanation. Isabelle concluded tentatively that it was simply her senior's way of dealing with too much to do in too little time. Then Sister Boucher pounced. 'There is a problem?'

'Oh, no! No, I was just wondering, that's all. I met Dr Chapuis at Madame Seguin's bed, you see.'

'Yes, Dr Ransan deputised him to decide on the new drug regime for Madame Seguin. Her son told us that the side-effects were upsetting her. It's a pity when patients don't tell us these things themselves.' Madame Seguin's son. The tall man? 'Let's hope her nausea will subside now.'

'I'll ask her about it later on.'

'And now...'

'Yes, Sister Boucher?'

Another six hours of hectic activity followed, punctuated

only by a lunch-break which most of France would have considered lamentably brief. At three Isabelle was due to go off after handing over to the next shift with a detailed description of each of her patients and what needed to be done for them. Thinking, with a longing born of considerable fatigue, about her neat, cosy little apartment overlooking the River Loque, a restorative cup of coffee and a snack—and perhaps a gossipy chat with Madame Claire— it was very tempting to hurry off right on schedule.

There was, however, a proverb applicable to this situation—a stitch in time...

Some of those unfamiliar forms she had filled in today, and the notes and reports she had made, could do with a review. Accordingly, she found some spare desk space in the quietest corner of the nurses' station and plunged into her paperwork, so determined to get through it quickly and efficiently and at the same time absorb everything of importance that she didn't even notice the comings and goings of the afternoon staff.

Until she became aware that someone was whispering to her. 'Nurse? Nurse! *Nurse!*'

She looked up, flustered and startled. Yes, he *was* talking to her—the tall, almost lanky man in the light-coloured suit, sitting in a wheeled swivel chair that looked far too small for him and writing up notes as assiduously as she had been doing. She hadn't even noticed his arrival, and felt a sudden unwelcome inrush of this morning's discomfort. She'd wondered earlier if he was Madame Seguin's son but now it was clear that he was a doctor, and that was his white coat flung over the back of the chair, getting crushed by the weight of his strong torso.

'Yes?' she whispered back to him.

'Madame Seguin's chart isn't in the rack,' he explained, again in a whisper. 'Are you working on it, by any chance?'

'I did have it earlier,' Isabelle whispered in answer. 'I

put it back. Technically, I'm off duty now so maybe one of the other nurses...'

'Yes, of course. I'll ask,' was all he said, barely voicing the words at all.

'I don't think you need to whisper.' She ventured to speak a little more loudly. Could the man be new? He seemed to have an exaggerated notion of patient confidentiality. Wearing those tortoiseshell-rimmed spectacles and an air of serious absorption in higher matters, he didn't *look* new, but... 'I'm sure Madame Seguin can't hear,' she further reassured him.

'Yes,' he acknowledged patiently and very hoarsely, 'but, since I have laryngitis, I have little choice!'

'Oh.' She blushed, feeling like a fool yet again, and now that she took a good look she could see that his nose was a little red and so were the very thickly lashed, very warm brown eyes behind those intellectual glasses. He didn't, in fact, look very well at all, although he appeared to be exercising a quite heroic mastery over his symptoms. And that surgical mask bearded below his jutting chin was even now being pulled into position so that he could keep his infection to himself as he moved around the ward.

'I must find that chart...' he mouthed, and only the faintest of sounds emerged through the mask, despite a tremendous effort of the vocal cords.

Uncurling himself from the swivel chair and more than confirming this morning's impression of his height, he strode off, coughing into his mask, and Isabelle, who felt horribly certain that she had put two and two together to make four, rather than six, this time, darted nimbly across to look for the name badge that would be pinned somewhere near the left lapel of that crumpled coat.

She found it, read it—and, yes, it *did* say Dr Jacques Ransan—and she still had the coat gripped in her hands when her grandmother's brother's grandson appeared before her again to rasp, reproachfully and briskly as he pulled down his mask, 'You didn't need to do that, you know. I would have told you.'

'I—I wanted to save you the effort of using your voice,' she manufactured inanely, dropping the coat over the back of the chair again and sidling awkwardly in the direction of her own seat.

'Canadian?' he smiled suddenly, ignoring her pitiful explanation. He had a very large smile which came and went quickly on his face, revealing teeth whitened by their contrast with his olive skin. He wasn't handsome, exactly, was her uncertain conclusion. Not *exactly*...With those spectacles he looked quite fearsomely intellectual, which wasn't generally an adjective that teamed easily with others such as 'hunky' or 'sexy'. And his features lacked the smooth regularity which made Remy Chapuis so repulsively certain of his own effect on women, and yet...

'Yes, I'm Canadian. From British Columbia.' And I'm your second cousin, only for some reason...I've forgotten it for the moment...I'm not going to tell you that yet. Oh, that's right. I promised Madame Claire...

'Welcome to France, then, and to Vesanceau,' he mouthed. He had his head slightly tilted to one side, as if straining to hear a distant, familiar melody that he couldn't quite catch.

'I— Thank you.' Are we really related? There's something about you... That melody. She was listening for it, too, now, with a tiny frown, just like his, etched between her brows.

'And do you like our Hôpital Saint-Jean so far?' he asked after a moment.

'Um, oh, yes, of course.'

He might have lost his voice, but she was the one who had lost her wits. He waited for a minute, with an air of cheerful patience, for her to come up with something a little more scintillating in the way of a response, but her normal ability to produce bubbling conversation whenever it was required seemed to have totally deserted her. He gave up in the end, as well he might.

That melody must have faded, too, because he coughed once, rubbed a thumb and forefinger against each temple, and turned back to the desk to open the patient's chart he had found, as if troubled no longer by elusive tricks of the mind. Perhaps the whole phenomenon had merely been the effect of his illness…or her imagination.

He worked on the chart and several other papers with full concentration for several minutes and seemed unaware that Isabelle still sat across from him, exuding all the panache of an unwanted hors d'oeuvre alone on a plate.

He's nothing like I imagined he'd be at all, Isabelle was thinking fuzzily. And I don't think he's how I wanted him to be. It's…it's getting too complicated. But why should I feel that? And why do I feel so…?

She didn't even have a word for it—in either of her fluent languages. Woolly-witted, she tried to focus on her notes again, but they all made so little sense that she was on the point of giving up. Then the unmistakable sound of Sister Boucher's bustling footsteps sounded behind her and there was a crow of solicitous disapproval.

'Dr Ransan, you are *not* supposed to be here today! You have sneaked in, I notice, thinking that I would have gone home, but unfortunately for you I was forced to stay late and you have been found out! I hope you have the sense to stay away from my patients in your condition!'

'Of course, and I have washed my hands a hundred times in the last hour,' came the hoarse reply, 'but, *madame,* my head is pounding…'

Sister Boucher merely moved in for the kill at this news.

'Ah! There you are, then! And what medicines have you taken for it?'

'None, I admit.'

'I thought so!'

'There really hasn't been time.'

'Time? I will get you some at once.'

'No,' he insisted. 'First get me someone to write down these notes while I close my eyes and dictate. The words are throbbing on the page when I try to steady my pen. And then I assure you I will be the most zealous invalid who ever lived. I will shut myself in my darkened apartment and admit no one, but no one—except my mother who announced by phone earlier that she is bringing me soup—until late tomorrow afternoon. Will that please you?'

His smile came again, an expression which told Isabelle very clearly that he was actually far more in control of the situation than a man this ill had any right to be.

'Hmm.' She heard Sister Boucher's sceptical snort. 'Someone to take your dictation—Isabelle!'

And so it was that she found herself scribbling down his rapidly whispered words about this morning's new admission, Yvette Chaillet, and her complex and as yet undiagnosed complaint, not daring to ask for hints as to the spelling of the more obscure French medical terms and giving herself aching fingers rather than tell this disturbing second cousin of hers that he was speaking far too fast in his non-existent voice.

She had a scant three seconds every now and then to notice the way the lashes of his closed eyes rested against his cheeks once those tortoiseshell spectacles were gone, and no time at all to wonder about how his voice would sound when he didn't have laryngitis. When his faint, rasping speech halted ten minutes later he gave a voiceless groan and replaced the spectacles, squeezed his temples between his large palms and told her weakly, 'Put the charts back where they belong, and put the notes in my bag. If

Sister Boucher wants to give me pills, I'm now fully prepared to take as many as she's got!'

He smiled and winced and groaned again as he stood up,
the hoarse sound reminding Isabelle of the voice of the
Creature in a very B-grade horror movie she had once had
the misfortune to see. Wishing that *she* had pills for him—
strong, oblivion-producing and very chemical pills, if that
was what he wanted—she could only smile sympatheti-
cally—dizzily—at him and send him on his way to seek
out Sister Boucher with a little pat on that long, strong
back.

He tilted his head and gave a small frown at the unexpected moment of contact, echoing Isabelle's own inner
question, Now, why did I do that? It was crazy! Then he
was gone, his lazy, loping stride extremely efficient although far too loose to be considered athletic. Behind him,
once again, he left just the suggestion of an elusive, familiar
melody, too distant to name.

Isabelle did as he had asked with charts and notes, waited
an uncertain moment, heard Sister Boucher scolding the
poor man again in the tiny kitchen area on the subject of
taking a decent amount of water with his pills and decided
to leave. Clearly, she wasn't going to get anything more
done here. Equally clearly, Sister Boucher had the situation
well in hand.

Isabelle herself could not make such a claim. When
Claire Oudot waylaid her on the way up the stairs of her
new home and pulled her into the apartment for a lavish
goûter of hot chocolate and pastries, she allowed herself to
be petted and fussed into a semi-reclining position on the
sinfully comfortable chaise longue, although she knew perfectly well that a charming but very thorough interrogation
was to follow.

It did.

Who were her patients? No *names,* of course, because

Claire knew almost everybody and it would be unethical to hear the intimate details of the illnesses of her friends…or her enemies. But surely just a few colourful anecdotes about certain ailments? And the staff? Was there a gorgon in charge of the ward? Did the doctors overstep their bounds? Were the juniors silly and flirtatious? 'Nobody *died* for you today, my poor dear, I do hope!' And finally, 'And did you encounter my dear Jacques?'

'I did, but only briefly.' She had considered a blatant lie on this subject but at the last minute it wouldn't come.

'Briefly!' Madame Oudot spat out the word dismissively. 'You can't tell me that it was too brief for you to form an impression.'

'Well, he had laryngitis…'

After a murmur of sympathy this, too, was dismissed.

'I had to take some notes for him, and that was really about it,' Isabelle insisted.

It was no excuse, it seemed. And she knew that she was lying. Madame Claire seemed to know it, too.

'One can tell a lot from such things,' she decreed. 'Just the turn of a phrase, the angle of a jaw. In the past, with a man, I have always known within three minutes whether I— But there! We're not speaking of me, are we? We are speaking of Jacques. Now, did you…remember what you promised me the other day?' Beringed hands twisted together in her lap. 'Did you tell him who you are?'

'Of course I didn't, Madame Claire. As you said, I'd promised I wouldn't. And I keep my promises!' Even when they're extracted with a degree of emotional blackmail!

There was a flash of something in Claire's eyes at these words. Relief? Isabelle didn't pursue the issue. In fact, she wanted very much to talk about anything other than Jacques Ransan.

Which was strange when her thoughts were brimming with him. That tall, loose-limbed frame… Odd that it should have struck her so when she'd always gone for the more compact, obviously athletic type. Those intriguing brown eyes, not quite as dark as her own, which she'd barely even glimpsed behind their intellectual glasses. A voice which she'd heard only in a strained whisper, dictating medical notes, a conversation completely crippled by her own lack of wit and the all-too-likely probability that he thought her a brazen flirt after his discovery of her *in flagrante* with Dr Chapuis...

'But one thing I *do* know,' she told Claire, with quite a hint of defiance, 'you're wrong to have frightened me about his reaction. When I tell him who I am, whenever that turns out to be, he's going to see things *my* way!'

'Ah! The eternal optimism of the young!' Madame Oudot said with an indulgent smile.

CHAPTER TWO

THE eternal optimism of the young seemed to have gone on strike when Isabelle arrived at work three days later after taking the now-familiar route on foot through the cobbled streets. She hadn't seen her second cousin in the intervening time—'He's taking my advice and staying in bed,' Sister Boucher announced with steely satisfaction—but Remy Chapuis had been very evident whenever a chest specialist was needed.

He appeared to be under the continuing impression that Isabelle's ultimate capitulation to his silky advances was a foregone conclusion, and she had found that there was nothing like the constant need to avoid someone for making her familiar with the precise layout of this rather labyrinthine building. Stairwells, broom cupboards, visitors' bathrooms... She now knew them all.

Today, Sister Boucher announced that Dr Ransan would be back, 'talking once more, and no longer infectious,' and Isabelle immediately thought wildly, Oh, no! Couldn't he have taken the rest of the week? I'm not ready...

Which was distinctly out of character, and since she couldn't possibly attempt to avoid *him*, too...

I'll just behave quite naturally.

But what *is* natural? Somehow I've forgotten. Why?

And then, suddenly—a few minutes later—it wasn't a problem; it didn't matter; everything was fine. He came on his round while Isabelle was at Yvette Chaillet's bedside, taking her pulse. The stockily built sixty-eight-year-old woman was quite ill, and becoming more so daily, and in Dr Ransan's absence Dr Chapuis had ordered batteries of tests which had kept revealing new and worsening problems but had brought him and two other specialists no closer to a diagnosis.

Madame Chaillet had been asthmatic for most of her life and took regular medication, including steroids, to control this, but her general health had been good until very recently, apart from a bout of flu that had been making the rounds. Hitherto, her medical needs had been very adequately cared for by her local doctor.

Now, though, she was suffering from fever, weight loss, weakness and malaise. Her liver and spleen were enlarged, her lymph glands were inflamed and she had ulcers of the mouth and mucous membranes. There was evidence of gastro-intestinal bleeding, and blood tests had revealed insufficiency in the adrenal gland as well as a low platelet and white cell count.

Her chest symptoms, which had prompted the original decision to refer her to Dr Ransan and admit her to this ward, were reflected in the lung X-ray, which showed fluid in the lower parts of the lung, enlarged lymph nodes between the two major lobes, a scattering of white spots and signs that infection had infiltrated much of the lung area.

Simone Boucher had been heard to mutter that if Dr Ransan didn't recover soon then Madame Chaillet certainly wouldn't. And now, recovered or not, here he was.

Remy Chapuis was with him, as well as Sister Boucher and a small clutch of medical students—one of whom was such a stunning redhead that it was immediately clear that Dr Chapuis's attentions would no longer be a gauntlet for Isabelle to run. Indeed, he was eclipsed at once by the simple elements of a quick smile, brown eyes and some calm, good-humoured words, 'Ah! Mademoiselle Bonnet, who was good enough to take my notes the other day when my temperature was making the mercury erupt through the top of the thermometer!' So this was his voice! A dark, vibrant tenor, still a little scratchy, in between cadences that were pure velvet. 'Can you tell us about this patient, please, Dr Chapuis, while Mademoiselle Bonnet finishes her observations?'

Their eyes met as he spoke, but the light reflected off his glasses and she couldn't quite see those brown orbs. Once again he looked fearsomely intellectual, and she wondered why thinking about him, as she had been doing fairly frequently since Monday, had made her so unreasonably flustered.

Then he pulled at the tortoiseshell frames, dropped the glasses into his hands and began to polish the lenses with a tissue so that now she could see his curved dark brows, the soft skin at the corners of his eyes and the complex depths of his black pupils. The source of her flusterment— if that was a word—was suddenly clear.

'Talk about Clark Kent and Superman!' she muttered in English under her breath. 'Now I know how Lois Lane felt!'

Several pairs of eyes that *weren't* Dr Ransan's fixed politely and slightly confusedly upon her, and she quickly switched to French. 'Her pulse is ninety and weak, blood pressure 106 over 50 and temperature 38.6 degrees centigrade.'

'We are speaking of Yvette Chaillet,' Remy Chapuis came in pompously, 'whose diagnosis remains a mystery.' He ran through her endless list of symptoms with a degree of relish and drama that seemed exceptionally tactless, then added, 'And she can't seem to give us *any* indication of what she might have done to deserve all this! Can you, Madame Chaillet? Have you been consorting with lepers and rabid rats, perhaps?'

One of the medical students—*not* the stunning redhead—

tittered dutifully, but the rest just glanced rather uneasily at the patient, who was feeling too wretched to enjoy Dr Chapuis's scintillating humour. Dr Ransan seemed impatient with it, too.

'What Dr Chapuis has failed to mention,' he said with authority, 'is that Madame Chaillet is our very top priority on this ward at the moment. We don't enjoy a medical mystery like this, and we know it can be solved.'

His quick smile fell on the patient like warm, welcome summer rain, and she looked a little less tortured than she had just a moment before. There was something very reassuring about that intelligent confidence. Isabelle felt it at once, and she knew Madame Chaillet did, too.

The group was on its way again after more discussion, and Isabelle couldn't help watching Jacques Ransan's white-coated back as it moved out of the room.

He doesn't look athletic at all, and yet… How does such a tall man move so easily? Not stiff at all. Loose, but not in the least bit clumsy. And why do I find it so impossible to look away?

'*Mademoiselle! Mademoiselle!*' came a weak voice.

'Oh, I'm sorry, Madame Chaillet. You didn't have a question for the doctors, did you?'

'That Dr Chapuis didn't give me a chance to ask it if I had,' the elderly woman retorted, just a quavering thread of sound but with spirit nonetheless. She didn't speak much as her mouth ulcers made this a painful process, not to mention all her other discomforts.

'No, he didn't, did he?' Isabelle squeezed Yvette Chaillet's blunt, work-worn hand as she put the blood pressure equipment back on a trolley.

'And he made a joke, as if it's all my fault that I'm sick like this.'

'He needs to work on his bedside manner, that's for sure. But Dr Ransan will be handling most of your tests and treatments from now on...' If only we can find out what we're treating! '...and his bedside manner is much better, don't you think?'

'Oh, yes! He seems so nice, and he inspired my confidence...a *little*...' If this seemed to Isabelle like being damned with faint praise, she had to remind herself that a very ill elderly woman couldn't be viewing life very rosily at the moment.

There were several small eddies in the wake of Dr Ransan's departure from the ward half an hour later, and they combined with the eddies created by the other two rounding specialists to create considerable turbulence. Three patients had been pronounced ready for discharge, and two more were to go to a convalescent home. Someone else was arriving from Intensive Care now that her condition had stabilised, and Madame Chaillet herself was having another blood test, more sputum cultures, an initial dose of wide-spectrum antibiotics and a drug to reduce her fever.

Then, after lunch, things got really busy.

Isabelle took the phone call from Accident and Emergency. 'We're sending someone up. Acute asthma. She should have gone to Intensive Care but they're full. We've done a couple of things here for her but she's not responding well and Dr Ransan hasn't got here yet. We've paged him again and told him to come straight up to you. And there's an added problem...'

Both the patient and the added problem arrived a few minutes later. The first was an elderly woman who was dangerously blue around her mouth and extremities and struggling desperately for breath, clearly terrified and quite unable to speak despite the oxygen mask and intravenous drugs that had been started downstairs. The added problem was her small grandson, aged about two, who was tearful and confused and fighting to stay with *Grand-maman* at all costs.

Dr Ransan came charging along the corridor, white coat untidy on his long body, just as Sister Boucher shouted, 'Respiratory arrest! We need a doctor *now!*'

He didn't mess around, expertly passing a tube down the patient's throat, bagging air into her lungs and stepping up the flow of drugs through her intravenous line—drugs which needed to act quickly to ease the potentially fatal constriction in the complex folds of her lungs.

She was struggling to speak but the tube in her throat now made this impossible and she began fighting it, trying to tear it away. Dr Ransan ordered sedation and soon the unknown woman had relaxed and accepted the discomfort and restriction of the tube.

'That's looking a little better now,' he said at last, then looked around, his brown eyes narrowed and searching. 'But what's that smell? It's ammonia. The cleaners? It's as strong as an old cheese! It hit me as soon as I got here and it can't have helped this woman's tightness.'

In the drama no one else had noticed it, but now Sister Boucher sniffed suspiciously as well. 'Ammonia? Yes, good heavens!' She bustled into the corridor and gave the benefit of her tongue to a rather apathetic-looking young woman desultorily sponging up the bottle of cleaning fluid she had spilled some time before.

The woman only shrugged. 'I couldn't get to it earlier. Some nurse called me to wipe up a spilled bedpan. More important, wasn't it?'

'As it happens, no!' Sister Boucher rasped.

The cleaner shrugged again. 'Well, I didn't know, did I?'

Then Dr Ransan took a single step towards the door. 'Do you realise we have a patient here on the verge of death, partially because of you?'

There was an electric moment, and at last the cleaner

was spurred to a more efficient response. 'Shut the door! I'm cleaning, OK? I don't want to see her die!'

'Yes, shut the door,' Dr Ransan ordered quietly, turning away to bend over the patient again. 'And open the window. Those fumes are still strong and she's still touch and go. I'll speak to that cleaner's supervisor later! This patient should be in Intensive Care but they're full, I understand. Simone, ring for a relief nurse to augment your numbers here. This one should be closely monitored for several more hours at least.'

'I'll ring, but you know how it is, Dr Ransan. It's possible no one may come. Almost three o'clock already...'

'Nonetheless, you must try. We still have no idea who she is, do we?'

'No, there was no medic-alert bracelet, and no one has understood what she's tried to say. Not French, I think.'

'We're working in the dark, then, with no information on the pattern of her attacks.'

'I can stay,' Isabelle offered, still watching the readouts on the monitor and preparing to listen to the patient's chest again.

Sister Boucher didn't waste time with polite protests. 'You can? Excellent! For the full shift? If you can special this patient then Valerie will have her full complement to handle the rest of the ward.'

But Dr Ransan was a little kinder. 'You may get away earlier,' he said. 'I'll be back to check on her before dinner, and by then we may be able to get her into Intensive Care.'

Then there was a noise from the corner of the room and all three of them remembered the little grandson, evidently so overwhelmed by what had been happening that he had stopped crying and had shrunk into the most unobtrusive place, too terrified to make a sound.

'*Salut, mon garçon,*' said Jacques Ransan quietly, and

there was a crack from one trousered knee as he bent his long legs to reach the small boy's level.

'*Grand-maman*,' came the ghost of a whisper.

'Poor little thing,' murmured Sister Boucher. 'But, you know, Valerie is waiting for my report. What on earth shall we do?'

'Let me see if we can arrive at an answer. I have a little time now,' Dr Ransan said, and Simone Boucher slipped from the room, already cataloguing aloud the many things she needed to tell her counterpart on the incoming shift.

'*Grand-maman* is going to be better very soon, little man,' the doctor went on. His voice was getting hoarse again, but its tone was very gentle. 'It was frightening just now, I know, and we didn't have time to tell you what we were doing, but now you can see she is all safe in bed and she can breathe again, but she can't talk yet, so can you tell us your name?'

'Nicolas,' came the tiny reply.

'Just Nicolas?'

'Yes.'

'Are you French, Nicolas?'

'No… Yes, I'm French.'

'Is *Grand-maman* French?'

'Yes, she's French now. She used to live far away.'

Dr Ransan rose, turned to Isabelle and shrugged. Somehow his large hand had taken the little boy's small brown paw and was chafing it gently, grubby fingernails and all. 'He can't be more than two. I'm not going to pester him for more when he obviously doesn't know. She had no purse with her? No companions, obviously…'

'Nothing, as I understand it,' Isabelle told him. 'She was in the playground just across the river, playing with him, when the attack must have overtaken her.'

'It's windy today and that playground is dusty as we haven't had rain. Perhaps it was that, and the effort of keep-

ing up with him. Two-year-old boys can be quite energetic,
I understand.'

'So I've been told,' Isabelle agreed. Was that a twinkle
in his wonderful eyes, or just the light reflecting on his
glasses? And wasn't that the ghost of a sweet, familiar melody playing somewhere? She continued, gathering her
thoughts with difficulty, 'Evidently she struggled on, hoping it would go away, and by the time she needed help she
was too ill to make herself understood. A young mother,
there with her own child, called the ambulance and obviously Nicolas was brought in, too. Where's *Maman*,
Nicolas, do you know?' she asked gently.

Mistake. 'I don't know.' Large blue eyes brimmed.

'She'll be here soon,' Dr Ransan said firmly. 'And she'll
be cross with me if she finds out I haven't given you anything to eat or drink, Nicolas. So I'm going to do that right
now while you wait here with Nurse Isabelle.'

And she was so busy wondering just how he could make
her name sound that way—liquid, musical, warm—that she
almost missed the communication in his steady look.
Belatedly she realised that he wanted her to take the boy.

So she did, picking up the warm, sturdy little form and
finding that it settled on her hip in a way that felt quite
natural as she swayed gently in a soothing rhythm. Dr
Ransan evidently approved. He nodded, and that quick
white smile came and went, intriguing her once again.

'But if she...doesn't?' she murmured to him, a little
alarmed by his promise to the child.

'If I'm any judge, he'll be asleep before I can get back
with his milk and banana,' he mouthed. 'And, with all the
upset, he may stay that way for two or three hours, which
buys us some time. In fact...' He put a finger to his lips—
a long brown finger, fine firm lips, just a touch crooked—
and she looked at Nicolas.

'Yes...'

The tear-swollen eyelids were heavy and drooping and the child's head was beginning to loll against her shoulder as she swayed.

Dr Ransan glanced at their as-yet-unknown patient, then back at Nicolas. 'Let me…' Very carefully, he bent a little to slide one long arm between Isabelle's own body and that of the now-sleeping child, then his shoulder nudged softly against her breast as he gathered the boy into his own arms. She felt the fabric of his white coat, caught a faint whiff of nutty male scent and had her cheek tickled by a strand of his hair.

It only lasted a moment, but there was something very intimate about the silent transfer of that warm little form. The way they'd had to touch and accommodate each other's movements, the pressure of his shoulder as he'd lifted Nicolas, the way he'd bent to match her own lesser height.

This is ridiculous, she thought. My knees have gone weak. I never knew that really happened.

'How is her air moving now?' he asked, and Isabelle went quickly on her wobbly legs to the patient's bedside to listen through her stethoscope again and check a special instrument that read the patient's carbon dioxide levels.

'Slight improvement.'

He nodded.

'What are you going to do with Nicolas?' she asked softly, quite hypnotised by the sight of such a tall man holding a child so tenderly and carefully.

'Sit here, if I may, until he's thoroughly asleep.' He mouthed the words softly so that she had to watch each firm movement of his lips. 'Then… Well, I have a lecture to give at four. If you could get some pillows and a blanket we can rig up a bed for him. He should stay here, don't you think? In case he wakes, or in case some relatives turn up.'

'Yes, that sounds best,' she agreed, thinking fuzzily, Why am I *breathless* now? This is getting worse and worse!

So he manoeuvred himself carefully into a low chair by the bed, looking horribly uncomfortable with those long limbs stuck out everywhere. He made no complaint, though, and a soft expression on his face kept drawing her gaze each time she had a moment to spare from her vigilant watch over the elderly woman.

There weren't many such moments. The patient's eyes had drifted open now and she was fighting the sedative and the tube, trying to speak and gesturing at the sleeping Nicolas anxiously.

'I know you want to tell us who you are and how to get hold of Nicolas's parents,' Isabelle said in French.

There was a frustrated rasp, choked off by the uncomfortable tube in her throat.

'You're not French, are you?'

A small negative movement.

'English?'

Again, no.

'If I bring you paper and a pencil, could you write down a phone number for us, and a name?'

Frustration again, and incomprehension.

Isabelle tried very slowly. '*Numéro de téléphone? Nom?* Write down?' She mimed the action and got a positive response at last, but even this small activity and stress had worsened the patient's breathing once more so that paper and pencil had to wait while the respiratory rate was changed and her position altered a little at Dr Ransan's quiet suggestion.

'But now I must go,' he said when this was done. 'And, as I had hoped, he's still asleep so I need those pillows.' His strong chin was resting lightly on the child's soft hair.

From the bed came the grandmother's anxious gesturing,

and Jacques understood. 'You want him with you? Yes, there's room at the foot of the bed.'

It was a little unorthodox but it seemed to allay their patient's anxiety, so, when Isabelle had placed a pillow there, Jacques rose and gently heaped Nicolas into position with large, tender hands. His grandmother was a small woman and there was plenty of room.

'Good luck!' the doctor mouthed to Isabelle, and was gone a moment later, loping down the corridor with an easy stride.

He did not appear again for three hours, during which time the elderly patient, whose name turned out to be Mariana Descalu, wrote down her daughter's phone number, and a relieved young woman with a Rumanian accent soon arrived to find her little Nicolas still asleep at the foot of his grandmother's bed.

'*Maman* speaks no French,' Nadia Bouvet confirmed. 'She lives with us now, but it's only been a few weeks and she is still very unfamiliar with things here. I left her at the playground to go shopping, but I didn't realise she didn't have her inhaler with her. The wind must have blown the dust up, and Nicolas would have had her dashing about. She must have been frightened, and that only made it worse.'

'You must get her a medical alert bracelet,' Isabelle suggested, 'so that bystanders or emergency staff know her condition even if she can't explain.'

'Yes, we must. *Maman?*' She turned to her mother, who was still unable to speak because of the tube in her throat, and addressed her rapidly in Rumanian. The elderly woman nodded, and Madame Bouvet said in French again, 'We'll be more careful in future.'

Just then Nicolas stirred and opened his eyes, and was soon cradled in his mother's arms, clinging to her desperately for a few minutes and then putting it all behind him with a child's rapid powers of recovery so that he was chattering brightly and trying to run into all the rooms by the time his mother was ready to leave.

Things were much quieter after this. Madame Descalu was content to rest now that she knew Nicolas was safely with his mother, and this helped to improve her condition to the point where Isabelle wondered if Jacques would be happy with a less intensive level of care.

He returned at seven, wearing a dark suit and the aura of a fresh shave, as she was laying down the stethoscope after listening to her patient's chest again…listening to her chest but thinking about *him*, as it happened, once she'd satisfied herself that those breathing sounds were continuing to improve. As he'd taken her by surprise, she blurted rather inanely, 'How did your lecture go?'

His answer was serious and seemed a little absent-minded as he drew her to the open doorway. 'It went well, I think, though I'm not convinced they quite grasped my point about chest drainage.' Then he brightened. 'But only four of them fell asleep!'

She choked. '*Only* four?' She peeped up at him doubtfully through her lashes, and saw that he meant it. 'Oh…'

He caught her expression and explained gloomily in that dark tenor voice, 'Yes, I'm very boring, you see. It must be that, though some of my colleagues refuse to take the blame for the phenomenon in their own classes. They claim that it's fatigue on the part of the students.'

'Shame on them!' she ventured. He *was* teasing, wasn't he? 'To look for excuses like that!'

He pressed his arm against the doorway, looking as if he could easily support the entire structure. 'Exactly, although medicine is very hard, as you know, and it's true that anyone who wants to pass must study until the early hours and be ready for lectures again first thing next morning. But I like to set my sights high and, as you say, not look for these excuses. I've vowed that one day I'll keep an entire class awake for the full two hours, even if my subject is the anatomy of the pleural cavity!'

He watched her, not quite but almost smiling, and she glared at him, shaking her head. 'I don't know what to think. I really don't!'

'Well, perhaps you could cogitate more effectively over dinner,' he suggested calmly.

'Over dinner?' she could only echo her second cousin's words foolishly. 'With…?'

'But of course "with"! And perhaps by the end of the meal you'll be able to tell me if my sleeping students have a point.'

'Oh, I can't imagine you're boring,' she answered frankly. 'I blame the students completely!'

'Good.' There was a flash in his eyes that zapped her somewhere in the region of that pleural cavity he'd been talking about, and suddenly that deceptive aura of vagueness was quite gone. A deliberate chimera, she now saw. 'So you'll meet me at Chez Gabotte in the Rue Pasteur at eight o'clock. Or should I call for you?'

'I— Well, I can't,' she pointed out, and knew that there was relief in her tone. With her secret knowledge of their relationship, which Claire had made her promise not to share, this was moving too fast. 'Madame Descalu,' she reminded him, knowing he'd seen her reluctance. He was frowning, as if he were trying to read something that should have been familiar and had found that it wasn't.

'Yes,' he nodded, and when he straightened and stiffened a little she realised that they both must have been bending towards one another, unaware of it. 'But that's not a problem.' His tone was very medical now. 'I've already arranged to have her transferred up to Intensive Care. We still know too little about her condition to risk softening our approach. I'm going to keep her intubated overnight, and take a full history tomorrow. I've arranged for one of my students—not one who sleeps in class—to interpret for me. She is of Rumanian parentage, speaks the language fluently and is aware of medical practices there. That way we'll avoid any mistakes. Uh…'

He took off his glasses and polished them absently with his suit sleeve. 'But you would rather dinner was…'

She seized quickly on the excuse he was offering her, totally confused about her own mixed reaction and deeply regretting that promise to Claire. 'Yes, another night. I—I'm tired, and—'

'And if, after all, I were to put you to sleep, as well as my students…'

'You wouldn't.' She stumbled awkwardly over the words. 'I'm sure you wouldn't.' Why was she answering him seriously like this? She *knew* he was teasing! Somehow, though—possibly because her knees were acting like cooked spaghetti again—she just couldn't come up with anything remotely sensible *or* appropriately silly.

He shrugged in very Gallic fashion, as disappointed in her response as she was, perhaps, and their exchange ground to an uncomfortable halt.

Isabelle was wondering how long it would be before the hot dew of perspiration on her brow collected into crude beads of sweat and actually began to stream down her face. And Jacques was standing there, reading her mind like a child's picture book. Or that was how it felt.

His effect on her was getting more difficult to bear by the minute. This maddening sense of recognition, this horrible fluttering of her pulses, this distracting sense of her own femaleness, this itchy, throbbing desire to reach out and explore him with her fingers…and her lips.

And he *knew* it, didn't he?

He was experiencing a powerfully male version of the same thing, she sensed, so here she was confusing them both, denying it all by pleading 'tiredness' as an excuse for knocking back dinner. No wonder he looked more distant now.

The one thing to be relieved about was that his mind-reading abilities could not possibly extend to his knowing *why*. In fact, she hardly knew why herself. Yes, he was her second cousin, and when she'd cheerfully decided to engage his assistance in bringing her parents back into the Ransan family fold she hadn't even considered the possibility of this...this...*thing* between them. This sense that they were both listening to the same faint, familiar tune.

But it was a bonus, wasn't it? He couldn't shrug off her peace-making mission as unimportant if they themselves were defying the long-time family feud by—

OK, put on the brakes! Second cousin or not, and discounting the effect of imaginary melodies, she barely knew the man. Perhaps she'd wake up tomorrow not feeling like this at all. Perhaps it was all that French food—or the autumn air, or the sensual rhythms of her mother tongue—which kept making her feel she was living in the middle of a novel by Colette or Françoise Sagan.

'You *are* tired!' The innate authority had returned to his manner.

'Hmm?'

'There!' He pounced in quiet triumph on her vague answer.

'Well, yes,' she admitted. 'I've been on since seven this morning.'

'Sign off, then, while I see about transferring this patient upstairs, and then allow me at least to walk you home.'

'I—'

His fingertip came to her lips and rested lightly there and, since she hadn't a clue what she would have said, she capitulated to his gentle demand for silence.

'I will meet you down in the foyer in fifteen minutes as

there is one other patient I must see in the men's ward first. You'll be there?'

'Yes,' she nodded breathlessly, and there was absolutely no reason for her heart to be pounding the way it was. Get a grip, heart!

He took a bit longer than fifteen minutes. Twenty-two and a half minutes, actually, if she'd been counting. Which she wasn't, not *exactly,* only the clock sat right in front of her on the glossy cream-painted wall of the hospital lobby so how could she help it?

Standing up to meet him, she thought, I'm giddy. And breathless again. Why isn't there someone here to tell me he's not my type? Except when I look at him, I don't want to have a type anymore, unless it *is* him!

He took her arm and she gave a convulsive shiver. 'Cold?'

'No, just…'

'Perhaps, then…' He paused, swore and let her go rather abruptly to move some feet away as they emerged into the darkening evening. She turned to him with an alarmed question in her face, and he explained, 'Forgive me, but it suddenly occurred to me you might have classed me with Remy Chapuis.'

'Oh, Jacques, *no!* I mean, Dr Ransan.'

'Jacques is very nice…'

'Jacques…*is* very nice,' she agreed in a wobbly voice, tasting his name in her mouth. Soft chocolate? A salted cashew nut? Red wine? 'And, as for Dr Chapuis, I certainly haven't classed you—and I just hoped you hadn't classed *me*—after Monday in the store-room… It's such a cliché!'

He laughed. 'But I have quite an unshakable feeling that *you* are not a cliché, Isabelle.'

'Hope not,' she said meekly, thinking, Not a cliché but a bit of a coward, perhaps, because a part of me says I should tell him *now* that we're related, only divided by a family chasm, but I won't. I can't. I promised Claire. And I can't see how I'd find a way to say it now, anyway.

She had to keep reminding herself of all the very good reasons for her silence on the subject. Spoiling the mood. Biding her time. What she had promised Claire, and it was a promise which had now taken on the cast of urgency.

She remembered how very positive the older woman had been that Jacques would not be ready to forgive the past and, though in this she was still convinced that Claire must be wrong, she suddenly thought, He's capable of anger. I haven't seen it yet, but somehow I know. He doesn't *need* to bluster and yell the way Remy Chapuis does, because his authority and strength are much more real. He's not a weak man. Far from it. And if there was a good reason for him to be angry then it would be a frightening thing... *Could* there be? Perhaps I haven't been told the whole story.

'I can hear the cogs grinding,' Jacques said. 'What are you thinking, Isabelle?'

'Just...about family stuff.' True, as far as it went. Which wasn't nearly far enough.

'A long way from home, all of them?'

'Vancouver.' Not Quebec, where they'd started out in Canada thirty-five years ago, and thank goodness Bonnet was a common name!

'I've heard it's a lovely city,' he said.

'Yes, with the mountains and the sea. Vesanceau is beautiful...'

'I'm glad you think so.'

'Oh, I do! I have the loveliest view—over the river and the rooftops. The light sometimes on the stone of the buildings or shafting through the arches of the Pont L'Eveque and into the water... Actually, this is my place here.'

'Really?' He looked up at the lighted floors above the bicycle shop. 'But this is Madame Oudot's!'

'Yes, I—I rent the little apartment from her, the old *chambre de bonne* at the very top. It's why I have such a nice view, as I was just telling you.'

If he wondered why she was gabbling like this he didn't say so. *She* knew. It was guilt.

'I know her very well. She is an old family friend,' he was saying. 'A patient, too, occasionally, and a valued customer of my father's.'

'Oh, what does he do—your father?' She had to ask as it was a natural and obvious question.

In fact, it would have been rude not to ask it, but it felt like treading on dangerous ground. Or like starting off along the road to hell—taking a well-known route—the one that was paved with good intentions. This was the point of no return. She realised that if she was going to break her promise to Claire—tell him who she was—then now was the moment to do it. *Not* doing it meant that she had taken on Claire's caution and her willingness for intrigue along with that reluctant promise. She had another second or two at most to find the words if she was going to say them tonight…

'He owns a small cheese shop.'

'Oh, that's interesting,' she answered absently, still struggling with her uncharacteristic dissimulation. She hated keeping secrets…but she hated breaking promises, too.

'Actually, I doubt that he'd agree with you,' Jacques was saying. Isabelle's attention was caught by the sudden steel in his tone. Yes, she had known his capacity for anger was there, but why now?

She looked up at him sharply and caught the tension in his face, undiluted by the clear lenses of his glasses. He explained grimly, 'It isn't what he wanted to do with his life and he has a very sharp mind that has been wasted, through no fault of his own. I'm sorry, I don't know why

I'm telling you this when we scarcely know one another...
Except that I feel we *do* know one another—don't you?'

'Yes, I— It's weird, isn't it?'

'Weird?' he laughed. 'Wonderful, *I* think.'

'Oh, yes...'

'And on the strength of it...' He bent towards her, taking
her face softly between his warm palms, and brushed her
mouth with his lips. They were very soft yet firm in just
the right way, and her own lips parted slightly on an in-
stinctive in-breath—a little gasp of pleasure and awareness.
He was painting her mouth, it seemed, with brush-strokes
of desire. She felt the effect of his touch radiate outwards
into her limbs and plunge downwards into her very core.

The slow, tantalising kiss was over far too soon. He drew
his head gently away to leave her breathless, wanting more
but sharing instinctively what she knew he was feeling
too—that there was time.

'And now,' he whispered against her hair, stroking her
neck with his fingers, 'I will say goodnight because, fond
as I am of Madame Claire, I do not fancy coming under
her scrutiny just yet. She has an expensive taste in scandals,
and I don't intend this to be one...do you? It's our secret,
hmm?'

'Secret? Oh, Jacques, maybe it's best if I—'

'Sh! I see a curtain moving at the window. Sleep on this.'
That touch of his warm, dry fingers across her mouth
again—a gentle command. 'It will keep, I promise.'

Keep? she wondered, and was in quite a muddle of roads
to hell paved and tangled webs woven as she watched him
walk away, listening to that very French sound of his
leather shoes on the fan-shaped stone cobbles of the street.

CHAPTER THREE

'I DIDN'T know you smoked, Madame Claire,' Isabelle said.

The elderly woman was taking out a pack of exotic little cigarettes and an exquisite silver lighter, set with sapphires. She paused in the action, holding both cigarette and lighter with a delicate, practised gesture. 'I won't if you don't wish it, my dear.'

'Oh, no, feel free.' She waved a hand. 'Other people are.'

'You're kind! I know it's a nasty habit but I've had it since I was fifteen—I started at the beginning of the war, and smoked much more heavily then—and it's terribly hard to break.'

She inhaled with a mixture of grace and guilt, and puffed out a tendril of pale blue smoke into the restaurant air, in which a dozen fragrances of food, perfume and tobacco already jostled for prominence on this busy Saturday night.

'As for why you didn't know,' she went on. 'I don't at home. Again, habit. My good friend some years ago refused to let me. He said it made the curtains and bed linens smell, and he was right, of course.'

'Well, I appreciate his concern for your furnishings, but how about your health?'

Claire Oudot dismissed this. 'Too late to be worrying about that. It was *good* for my health in the war, soothing one's anxieties. People forget that, and of course then the health risks weren't fully known. Now... Well, it's a de-mon, true, but I'm lucky. It makes my colds worse in winter, that's all. Your cousin Jacques scolds me about it. I was in hospital last January for a few days.'

'In hospital? With a cold?'

'Well…' she looked a little guilty and put out her cigarette as a delectable quail in a fragrant gravy was set down in front of her '…I call it a cold. Why make a fuss? Your cousin Jacques says it was bronchitis and that, in effect, I always have bronchitis now—chronic. But I only notice it when I'm sick so why call it by some frightening name?'

'Oh, Madame Claire, it doesn't matter what you *call* it!' That explained the throaty quality to her voice that Isabelle had noticed. 'It's what it does to you. Can't you try to give up?'

A blue-veined hand covered Isabelle's as her own regional specialty of *truite au vin jaune* arrived. 'You're kind to care!' Claire's pretty blue eyes swam a little. 'Very kind. But if my cigarettes kill me so be it. Just as long as your cousin Jacques doses me up nicely so I don't feel any pain.'

'Please! Can you stop calling him that?' Isabelle blurted, goaded into the request after the third use of the phrase in as many minutes.

'Well, Dr Ransan, then, if you like. But he *is* your cousin.'

'*Second* cousin but, since you've made me promise not to tell him that yet, please don't keep reminding me…'

'Claire! I wondered if I'd find you here!' A rasping, laboured female voice spoke over Isabelle's shoulder and Madame Oudot's eyes lit up, as if she was as relieved at the interruption as was Isabelle. Neither smoking nor a certain pulmonary specialist were particularly comfortable topics of conversation.

'Jeanne! Can you join us?'

'Since otherwise I'd be eating alone, yes. I would have telephoned to suggest we meet, but I suspected you were still helping…' there was an odd hesitation '…helping your young friend settle in.'

Isabelle turned and smiled, though she had to hide a brief stab of shock at the appearance of the woman who had greeted Claire. Some years younger, perhaps about the same age as Isabelle's own mother, she had a horribly bent and bowed spine. Not osteoporosis, surely, since she must only be in her mid to late fifties. More likely a congenital malformation, unkindly known as crookback, which went by the medical name of kyphoscoliosis.

The flowing silk dress in autumn-toned florals, exquisitely draped though it was, could do little to hide the condition, but her exquisitely made-up face was truly beautiful and her dark eyes almost shouted their hunger for life so that Isabelle's attention was quickly distracted from the deformity.

Claire rose and the two women kissed, then introductions were made…and bombshells fell.

'My friend, Jeanne,' Claire began, then hesitated for a moment. 'Actually, Jeanne Ransan. She is Jacques's aunt and your father's cousin.'

Isabelle's jaw dropped. 'My father's cousin. You mean…?'

'I am François's twin sister, yes.' Jeanne nodded as she sat down, leaning one arm heavily on the table as she tried to make her posture as normal as she could. Her voice was thin and rasping, and Isabelle guessed that it was the effect of her malformed spine, which would significantly decrease her lung capacity and increase the effort needed to breathe.

'*Papa* never—' She broke off and bit her lip.

'Never mentioned me?' Jeanne finished with a complex smile, tilting her head to throw a wave of lustrous dark hair back from her face. 'No. We weren't close. My fault. I was a difficult young person to tolerate in those days. I like to think that things might be different if we were to meet again now. After all, I was your mother's good friend.'

She exchanged a look with Claire, and Isabelle again confronted the suspicion that Madame Oudot knew far more about the past than she was telling. Claire said, 'I told you, Jeanne, didn't I, that Isabelle has come to try and bring the family close again?'

'You did, indeed, and you also told me that my brother and my nephew are not to know of it yet. What do you think of this secrecy, Isabelle?'

'I'm not sure any more,' Isabelle answered frankly.

The waiter came and Jeanne quickly ordered something after a practised glance at the menu. Her choice of wine, too, spoke very clearly of expertise. This process gave Isabelle a short opportunity to weigh her next words. 'You must have an opinion yourself, Cousin Jeanne. My mother could have been your sister-in-law, and you'd have been my aunt instead of Jacques's. But haven't things worked out for the best? Where is the sense in resenting and re-gretting what happened thirty-five years ago?'

There was a rasping laugh. 'Claire has done her work well!'

'Oh, but those aren't Madame Claire's opinions. They're mine.'

There was another exchange of significant looks between the two older women and Isabelle was suddenly angry, though she was polite enough not to show it. Madame Claire certainly did like to act the puppeteer, pulling every-one's strings. Well, that chirpy charm, entertaining and en-dearing though it was, wouldn't work for ever!

I want some answers! Isabelle decided. Aloud, she said, 'Perhaps you can answer one question for me, Cousin Jeanne. Your nephew—and I'm sure you've heard all about the fact that we meet at the hospital almost daily!' She glared at Claire, who had the grace to blush. 'Your nephew seems very angry on his father's behalf—seems to feel that Cousin François hasn't been able to make the best of his life, and I wondered about that.'

'Eat up, Isabelle, dear,' Claire came in softly. 'Your dinner is growing cold and it looks so delicious! Mine is…'

'I *am* eating, Madame Claire, and savouring every morsel,' Isabelle replied firmly. 'But I can talk as well.'

'As to your father's cousin…' Claire went on.

'Can Cousin Jeanne—?'

'If I may speak for Jeanne?' Very deliberate and very sweet.

'I'm afraid the smoke is making me breathless,' the other woman said apologetically, and Isabelle could see that her breathing was more effortful than ever and her face looked very strained.

'Oh, and I was smoking earlier,' Claire said repentantly.

'Not just you—there are so many others.' Jeanne coughed behind her hand and shifted awkwardly in her seat. 'And to talk of François always makes me—'

Claire went on firmly, 'François had dreams of being a doctor himself once, but they were not realistic. Jacques doesn't realise that, of course. He was not yet even born when all this took place.' She waved her hand prettily.

'No, and neither was I so I wish you'd tell me something more than all this vague stuff, doctored with your own special brand of rose tint,' Isabelle said. 'I want the truth, Madame Claire!'

'Oh, my dear, what is *that*, I wonder?' Claire said, shaking her head.

Jeanne came in almost fervently, struggling to bring forth the words now, her lovely face tight, 'She's right, you know, *petite* Isabelle. Claire is as wise as a witch. She…' there was a desperate rasp '…cares about us so, and we all owe her far too much to question her viewpoint on this.'

Owe her? Isabelle wondered. And who, exactly, was

'we'? 'The more I find out the more there is to know,' she muttered in English, and she would have pursued the issue, except that Jeanne was clearly having real trouble now, working hard for every breath—and in pain as well, if Isabelle was any judge.

She was holding her left fist against her chest and had let her soup spoon drop to the table with a gesture of swan-like grace, ignoring the savoury bisque which had just been placed in front of her.

'Is it usual for you to feel like this?' Isabelle asked her newly discovered cousin gently.

'It is becoming so, I regret,' Jeanne gasped. 'With any exertion, or—or upset.'

'There's pain, isn't there?'

'Yes. It feels like…my heart. To tell the truth, I'm frightened… Before, it has been only mild, but tonight… Oh, I do hate to dwell on illness when life has so much else still to offer! And lately my ankles have been so swollen. At times my fingers, too, they've been like fat sausages. I told myself it was the summer heat, but that's over now and still I'm like this!' She laboured for breath once again.

'Oh, Jeanne, my *dear!*' Claire said, and her eyes swam with tears of concern, making Isabelle repent of her earlier anger. Claire might be a little too fond of stage-managing intrigues and scandals but she definitely cared, and there was something quite compelling about this beautiful woman.

'I think you need to see a doctor, Cousin Jeanne,' Isabelle said. 'Have you mentioned this to anyone? How long since you had a check-up?'

'Oh, not for… Well, when I was last in Paris, as I go to a man there. Six months? No, it's more… I've tried to forget about it, which is bad, I know. But until recently there was no pain, and nowhere near this *effort!*'

'I am phoning for a taxi, and I am phoning Jacques,'

Claire announced decisively. 'Then we are all going to the hospital together to meet him.'

'No, to bother Jacques on a Saturday night...' Jeanne pleaded.

'He is a doctor, Jeanne. It is his job.'

'And I'm a nurse. You need to be seen, Cousin Jeanne.' Isabelle added her own urging, taking her cousin's arm and sensing her tense, laboured effort to breathe and her cradling of the pain in her chest. She could see the swollen fingers, too, now that Jeanne had spoken of this problem.

There were no more protests, and the fear and effort in Jeanne's face increased. The fact that the three women proposed to leave most of their delectable meal uneaten signalled to the restaurant staff and the other diners that the situation was serious, and there was quite a bit of completely French, fairly useless and very endearing fuss over putting out cigarettes, opening the door and clearing a passage for Jeanne's exit.

During it all Isabelle heard someone whisper to a companion, 'That's Jeanne Ransan, you know, the Paris *couturière*. Yes, she's from here originally. You didn't recognise that marvellous face? She closed her salon several years ago and came back.'

It seems that strangers on the street know more about my own relatives than I do! Isabelle thought.

Then the taxi arrived, bucketing along the cobbled alley outside the restaurant with a self-important blaring of its horn. The driver continued to take his mission very seriously—quite alarmingly so, as far as Isabelle was concerned—as he rocketed across what was supposed to be the pedestrians-only Place de l'Horloge down a side street barely wide enough for two cars to pass and through a rear entrance to the hospital grounds.

Fortunately, the bar that prevented unauthorised vehicles from entry during the day was already raised, as Isabelle doubted whether the driver could have stopped in time if it had not been.

Accident and Emergency was fairly busy tonight. Isabelle noticed a heavily bleeding cut, a bicycle fall and a frail-looking old woman who probably had a fractured hip, each about to be treated while other patients and their families waited. She recognised the triage nurse from her own orientation two weeks ago and they greeted each other briefly. The nurse asked several questions, then handed Jeanne over to an orderly with a wheelchair.

He was about to wheel her away when Jeanne said hoarsely, 'Can't my friends come too? Isabelle is a nurse, and I don't want to be left alone.'

'Go on, yes, of course,' the triage nurse nodded.

Jacques Ransan arrived five minutes later while a junior doctor was still asking preliminary questions on Jeanne's history.

'Tante Jeanne…' He took her much smaller hands in his large ones and kissed her, but his eyes were on Isabelle, smouldering with a potent mix of pleasure and surprise that she could not miss. She only hoped that Claire's attention was on her sick friend.

'I'm so sorry to disturb you, Jacques,' Jeanne said. She reached up to give him a loving touch on his smooth, olive-skinned cheek.

'What nonsense!' he said. 'I am on call for such occasions as these, and I have been telling you for months that a Paris specialist—much as I esteem my colleagues in the capital—can't do you much good now that you are living in Vesanceau once more. *Bonsoir,* Madame Claire…and Mademoiselle Bonnet. Now, it's your breathing?'

'And my heart. I'm sure it's my heart. A pain right here.' She pressed her chest again, and Isabelle could see that her hand was trembling.

Jacques flicked his stethoscope into position and listened

carefully in several places as he instructed his aunt to breathe or hold her breath. He murmured something to the junior doctor who still stood in attendance, and then asked Jeanne, 'Have you been feeling more tired than usual of late?'

'I— It's so hard to say. That's what my man in Paris always asks. Yes. Yes, I have, but I try to keep fit and get about. Vesanceau is so beautiful at this time of year, and I must have my beauty! You know that, Jacques.'

'Yes, I do.' He supported her carefully as she clung to him.

'How can I give up on life when every detail of it is so precious to me? So, yes, perhaps I overdo it. Is that the reason for the swelling? And I—I fainted the other day as I went up the stairs after doing my shopping.'

He nodded, then bent to her more closely and took her hand again, chafing it. 'You know that I can't give you good news,' he said. 'You've lived with this back of yours all your life, and you've known that age would make it worse.'

'Yes, but that doesn't stop me from being scared, Jacques!'

'Of course it doesn't. Which is why you'll get the best care. We'll admit you now and we need a heart specialist to see you. The stress on your lungs is starting to affect your heart,' he explained. 'It has to work too hard, you see. It's complicated and I won't explain it all now. Our heart man, Dr Froissart, will do some tests, and I'll do a couple more myself. Not painful or uncomfortable ones. An X-ray of your chest, and an electrocardiogram.'

'Oh, I can deal with discomfort and pain, if it's all explained.'

'It will be. Now, Dr Froissart is very good, of course, or he wouldn't be at this hospital, and with a few days of rest and treatment we'll find a way for you to keep this under control once you're home again. Was it Mademoiselle Bonnet's idea to bring you in?' That glance flashed her way again.

'Yes, and Claire's. I—I had to be bullied a little.'

'I shall have to thank Mademoiselle Bonnet for her severity, then, because it's very good that you came in. It's nice to see a tenant so concerned for the health of her landlady's friends.' His mouth took on a teasing shape.

Isabelle burned at once and almost blurted the truth about her status in the lives of Jeanne and Claire, but caught Claire's eyes emitting what were almost *sparks* of warning.

Jeanne, meanwhile, was too ill to care about these nuances of truth and secrecy. 'I'm to be admitted to a ward. What will I do? I have none of my things, my toiletries and make-up.'

'Don't worry, Tante Jeanne. Madame Claire and I will get them for you now,' Jacques soothed. 'I have no other patients to see. Your apartment is not far, and by the time we get back you will be settled and I can give the orders for your care.'

'Isabelle, will you stay with me?' Jeanne groped with her swollen fingers to take her younger cousin's hand.

'Of course I will, Co—Madame Ransan!' But I hate this. I stopped just in time then. What can he be thinking?

She didn't dare to look at him to find out, and only hoped that her impression yesterday that he could see right into her thoughts was only a delusion born of—of—

Of the fact that I'm wildly attracted to him, she admitted to herself miserably. Claire didn't envisage *this* when she swore me to secrecy... Or *did* she?

The elderly woman was chirping, 'It's so good to see a really genuine vocation for nursing such as Isabelle has, isn't it, Jacques? So skilled and so willing!'

'Indeed,' he drawled. His glance flashed past so quickly

that she couldn't capture it, though she wanted to very badly.

'And so sincere in her desire to bring harmony between people, as I think you will find out when you get to know her better—which you will naturally do in the course of your work.'

'Come, Claire,' he responded, unperturbed by all this froth. 'We must collect Tante Jeanne's things for her, and the orderly is here to take her to the ward.'

Isabelle helped to transfer Jeanne to the wheeled stretcher and then they took the large lift up to the fourth floor, where the cardiac unit was situated. Jeanne was alarmed to find herself here, having expected to go to Isabelle's own ward where she had been two years ago with pneumonia and again last year with a bad bout of flu.

The reduced lung capacity caused by her spinal deformity laid her open to more severe attacks of any respiratory ailment and she was used to this, it seemed, but the heart ward was something new and loomed ominously.

'So it is a heart attack. I could die in the next minute, and he was just protecting me from the truth!' she exclaimed hoarsely, and it took Isabelle some time to quiet her fears once again. Jacques and Claire returned, in fact, while she was still answering Jeanne's laboured questions as best she could.

A resident on call for the ward appeared as well, and the two doctors conferred for several minutes before Jacques came back to the bedside and said, 'We're going to put you on oxygen therapy, Tante Jeanne, and a diuretic to reduce that swelling. We'll also use a drug to open up your airways a little more and, of course, something for the pain if you need it. But until Monday, when Dr Froissart will be doing his tests and conferring with me on the results, your main job is to rest and stop worrying.'

'And my job is to bully you into it if I have to!' Claire

said. 'I'm going to stay with you until you are sleeping, Jeanne, my dear.'

'No, but your meal, and Isabelle's, too.'

'Isabelle will have her meal. Jacques will take her, won't you, Jacques?' She didn't wait for his agreement. 'As for me, my dear friend, how can I go off and eat when you are like this?'

She squeezed Jeanne's hand, and again her palpable love for the woman forced Isabelle to forgive Claire for the wicked trick of virtually *ordering* Jacques to take her to dinner. He must be embarrassed and horrified.

Only he wasn't.

'Your landlady seems to share my own opinion about the importance of us getting to know one another better,' he murmured as soon as they were out in the corridor.

'She's a terrible woman!'

'Seriously, Isabelle?'

'Seriously, I'm starting to love her like mad, but there are moments. Oh, there are moments!'

He laughed, a rich tenor sound that came from deep within his taut diaphragm. 'Yes, she's been like a fairy godmother to my family, only we've never quite decided whether she's a good fairy or a bad one. What's your impression?'

'Oh, she's far too fascinating to be good, Jacques! That was obvious to me straight away!'

His car was parked outside in the area reserved for doctors. It was very quiet at the moment, with the classical domed roof of the original hospital a dim, elegant shape against the cloudless night sky and a crispness to the air that was invigorating even as it invited her to seek the warmth of an interior...or of someone's arms.

Jacques unlocked the passenger door, saying, 'She certainly seems fond of you.'

'Well, she has good taste, then, doesn't she, to augment her spicier virtues?' Isabelle teased.

'She does…' he murmured and, as if he'd been waiting for the opening, he turned her away from the car and pulled her against him.

The moment had been in the air between them since their last much briefer kiss. No, she amended with a flash of insight, since that ridiculous encounter at the store-room door when her skin had still been crawling from Remy Chapuis's unwelcome touch. Now it was Jacques who was holding her, they were alone and the feeling of his arms around her could not have been more different.

It was like coming home, like opening a door and hearing that elusive, familiar melody that had been nagging at the edge of her mind—not faint and far away any more but right here, played live by a full orchestra.

He felt the same, though how she could know that…

'I'm reading minds now, too,' she muttered in English, not even sure that she'd said the words aloud until he searched her expression with a soft smile threatening to break open on his face.

'Quoi?'

'Oh…nothing.'

'I speak some English, you know.'

'That wasn't English. That was…the language of my heart, I think,' was her dazed answer.

He had her hands in his and was stroking them with his thumbs. It was hypnotic and sent shivers chasing up her spine. They were standing length to length, but with him so tall and her so petite… She rose onto her toes, wanting to get closer to that delicious face—to explore its tanned and not fully symmetrical planes with her fingers.

He bent towards her, scooping handfuls of her wildly curling dark hair and tilting his head, then frowned and laughed. 'This is impossible! We need a stepladder for you. We are like a Percheron and a Shetland pony...'

'A Shetland? They're fat!'

'...or a giraffe and a little gazelle.'

'That's better!'

'We should give this up now, except...except...'

'That it's so nice,' she finished against his mouth because he had somehow managed to bridge the gap between them, or they both had, with her stretching like a child to reach forbidden sweets on a table and he so awkwardly bent.

It didn't feel awkward. He tasted faintly of caramel, it seemed to her. Caramel? No... Perhaps vanilla or hazelnut. Delicious, and as elusive as that phantom melody that seemed to play around him so that she kept kissing in order to explore further and come up with a better answer. And he was still scooping her hair into his hands, kissing it, now and murmuring about its fragrance, too.

'Almond?'

She laughed and nuzzled her face into the warm curve of his neck. 'Funny, I was thinking about nuts, too. That you tasted of hazelnuts.'

'Then you're hungry and I must take you to dinner, as I promised Madame Claire.'

'Oh, yes, I suppose so, but—'

'First, more of this...'

'Please. Lots more,' she breathed. 'Oh, that sounds so— I don't usually *lavish* myself upon—'

'I know you don't,' he said throatily. 'But something's got into my blood, I'm afraid. Some kind of fever that you've caught as well, and I'm ready to take every bit of this delight that you're offering...'

There was silence after this for some minutes. He nipped at her lower lip, drawing on its trembling fullness, then explored the shape of her mouth with his tongue until she threw back her head with a groan and lolled against the big hand that supported her back while he covered the length of her throat with his mouth.

Her fingers splayed to take his head in her hands, and she felt the silk of nut-coloured hair that was slightly too long and the delicious roughness of a jaw that had not been shaved since that morning. He touched his tongue to the skin beneath her tender ear lobe and she gasped.

Then a cry escaped his lips and she felt something hard fall against her jaw and clatter to the ground. At the same moment she cried out as well. Her calf was cramping after all that standing on tiptoe, and seconds later they were both bent double. She was grabbing at her painfully tightened calf and then at her instep, trying to stretch the cramp away, while he was saying urgently as he groped on the gritty bitumen of the car park, 'Don't move, Isabelle! My glasses are on the ground...'

And if the combination of these prosaic disasters wasn't the least romantic ending to a kiss she'd ever had...

'It's going. It's ebbing,' she gasped.

'Here they are, thank goodness! Now, are the lenses cracked or the frames bent? No... Oh, *nom de Dieu*, Isabelle, I'm sorry!'

Tangled together, they fell to a sitting position, he on the asphalt and she on his lap. 'Oh, Jacques, your suit...'

'I don't care about the cursed suit!' he growled. 'Nor the glasses, for that matter. You had a cramp. Are you all right?'

'Yes, it's gone now.'

'We must get some food into you.'

'It's all right.'

'It's not! This nonsense about kissing!' He nuzzled her ear as he spoke and tightened his arm around her. 'Don't you know what a Frenchman's priorities are?'

'You mean you haven't eaten either?'

'Oh, Isabelle, what a delight you are! Now, if only we could get you a milking stool…'

'A *milking* stool?'

'For you to stand on. If I lose my glasses whenever I bend to reach your mouth, and you get a cramp whenever you stretch, what future is there for us?'

What future, indeed!

I'd do it, too, Isabelle knew. If that was what it took, I'd carry a milking stool with me wherever I went!

LIFE TOOK ON the most delightful glow after that night. There was a magic to everything, an air of unreality, and if that last word contained ominous undertones then Isabelle shrugged them off.

Their meal together was wonderful. He took her back to the place where she had started the evening with Claire, and though it was now quite late the couple who owned and ran *Au Bord de la Loque* appreciated the importance of a tasty and nourishing meal after the drama of the evening and fed them like geese being fattened for Christmas.

They were eager to hear that Jeanne would be all right and Jacques softened his report, both to protect his aunt and to keep at bay any lavish protestations of sympathy. He and Isabelle both knew that the future would be hard for Jeanne if Monday's tests showed the expected picture.

The life-long compromise of her lung capacity had created heart damage that was irreversible—specifically the thickening and enlargement of the muscles on the right side, which were now failing—and the best that could be expected now was a small improvement in her condition by careful use of drugs and oxygen and a curtailed lifestyle.

'How hard will this news be for her?' Isabelle wanted to know.

'Well, she's seen it coming. She's known all along that her condition would limit her life expectancy, and she's lived her life accordingly. She had thirty very successful years in Paris, where her design talent brought her into the highest social circles, which she seems to have enjoyed enormously. Coming back home five years ago was an acceptance that she had started the process of dying, I think.'

'How much longer can her heart and lungs keep going?'

'It depends on how hard she's willing to fight. That heart pain tonight upset her. This man in Paris can't have told her clearly enough that her heart function might eventually be compromised by the strain on her lungs. And perhaps he was right not to worry her unduly in advance, when nothing could be done. It's not as if surgery was an option when she was a child, back in the late thirties and early forties. But one thing I do know...'

'Yes, Jacques?'

'If Tante Jeanne could hear us now, spending our first evening together glooming over her, she would be wringing her hands. Would you think me heartless if I say let's not talk about this any more tonight? Let's live as she has always lived, refusing to give in to it?'

'I think you're right, that it's what she'd want.'

And in the end they achieved it, with the help of the delectable food and wine and something less tangible—an immediate connection between them that made even their silences delightful. The restaurant was ready to close by the time they left, and it was almost midnight.

ON SUNDAY, with a misty rain falling, she carried out the lazy timetable he had teasingly wrung from her the night before. Sleep in...dreaming of his goodnight kiss, actually—which hadn't been part of the day's plans but came as a warm, syrupy bonus on her schedule—tucked beneath her white cotton quilt as the soft, rain-dulled dawn crept in. Have breakfast with Madame Claire. Write letters home.

Provision her little kitchen from the market across the bridge.

She visited Cousin Jeanne with Claire in the afternoon as well, and found her feeling a little better, the chest pain having subsided. That was good news, and Jeanne was in better spirits. On the way home the late sunshine came out which meant that she could go for a long walk by herself through the fascinating old town, window-shopping and— she had to admit it—daydreaming about Jacques.

ON MONDAY MORNING she saw him first thing as he came on a ward round just after she began work at seven. Sister Boucher, harried as usual, deputised her to trail along with the group of doctors and students.

'I'm sorry, Mademoiselle Bonnet, when you are so new but, sadly for my other nurses on this particular shift, you are by far the most competent and the most informed, and if you do get put on the spot—asked an impossible question or told to write something down that you can't spell—just be honest and tell them you don't know. Dr Ransan may *look* terrifying and formidable but, really, I assure you he's a very considerate man, not an ogre at all, and he won't bite your head off.'

'Thank you. I'll remember that,' Isabelle responded demurely, planning to report the whole conversation to Jacques himself that afternoon. He had a lecture to give at three, but at five he wanted to take her for coffee and cakes...

He was every inch the doctor this morning, she found, but in a way she was already beginning to think of as uniquely Jacques—earnest and very technical in his discussion of signs, symptoms, treatments and prognoses, but given to sudden, unexpected witticisms—delivered with such deceptive mildness that two of the young medical students never caught the jokes at all.

And every now and then he would take off those intimidating and intellectual spectacles, and she'd become aware
of the stunning Clark Kent to Superman transformation all
over again.

Their complement of patients had changed a little since
Friday. Madame Descalu was back from Intensive Care but
would be discharged today with a prescription for some
more up-to-date asthma drugs than the ones she had been
using. Madame Chaillet was still with them, still worsening
and still undiagnosed. There was beginning to be an ominous question mark hanging over her, hinted at by the
reams of notes, the frequencies of visits from several different doctors and the repeated changes in symptom-
relieving medications. Would this unknown complaint
prove fatal?

'She's such a nice woman—so rarely complains, puts up
with Dr Chapuis, hangs on every word from Dr Ransan,'
said Carine Faivre, who had nursed her on the night shift.
'We have to do something more for her!'

And there had been a new admission yesterday afternoon
from the convent of the Order of Claire nuns high up on
the hill beyond the Église Saint-Paul.

'Sister Marie-Pierre has pneumonia,' reported Remy
Chapuis, 'but she tried prayer instead of penicillin...' He
brayed with laughter at his own joke. No one else did. 'So,
of course, now she's pretty sick.'

'The patient is awake, Dr Chapuis,' Jacques warned in a
quiet and steely voice.

'Yes, I know, but I doubt she's—'

'Then perhaps we'll just ease ourselves into the corridor
here, Dr Chapuis...' he did so, and everyone followed '...if
wit is to be exercised at the patient's expense.' His voice
was not raised, but it had brought Remy Chapuis to a state
of gibbering apology nonetheless. Jacques merely waved
this away, then went on, 'She was a little confused yester-

day, as I understand it, but now she's oriented in time and place?' He turned to Isabelle, who had been assigned to Sister Marie-Pierre and given a report on her condition by her night-shift counterpart.

'Yes, she spent a good night and understands what has happened. Apparently, another nun noticed evidence of some confusion and disorientation yesterday afternoon and became alarmed. When she—'

'I'll continue, *mademoiselle*,' Dr Chapuis came in firmly, in an attempt to recoup his status after Dr Ransan's chastisement. 'She was started on oxygen and intravenous fluids, as well as an anti-inflammatory drug.' He consulted his notes briefly and named it.

'Why that particular drug, Dr Drouot?' Jacques asked one of the students mildly.

'Uh… It is effective without suppressing respiration.'

'And why is pain relief particularly important here?'

'Because pain discourages effective coughing, which we need—or the patient needs—in order to loosen the lung secretions.'

'Right, and in this case she is rather weak at the moment as well so the physiotherapist will be making regular visits to assist with chest drainage. Now, as Dr Chapuis so amusingly indicated to us a few moments ago, Sister Marie-Pierre was unaware that she was ill enough to need hospital treatment. The course of what is the most likely type of pneumonia in this case can be quite slow, not to say insidious and hard for the sufferer to detect, so now we have wasted no time, I hope, Dr Chapuis?'

'Antibiotics have been started, yes, pending the result of the sputum culture, at which point a change can be made if necessary, but what we have her on now covers the most likely cause of the disease, as you have said, Dr Ransan.'

'Good. Let's move on, then. Ah, one more thing, Mademoiselle Bonnet, that Dr Chapuis has so kindly reminded us of with his mention of prayer earlier...'

Leaning against the doorway, he bent towards her and she thought again of milking stools and stretching to reach his kiss. If that caressing twinkle in his brown eyes was any guide he was thinking of it too.

He said quietly, 'You may want to ask her if there's anything she wants brought in. Her rosary beads, perhaps, or a holy picture. She may not dare to ask but would fret, and I do like to look after our Claire nuns—whose forebears founded this very hospital—as they sometimes don't look after themselves as well as they should.'

'I think she's dozing again,' Isabelle said, glancing into the room, 'but I'll ask as soon as she's awake.'

The group moved on, and after seeing three more patients they left the ward. Isabelle was able to report to Simone Boucher when they had gone, 'No drastic mistakes, *madame,* I don't think.'

'Good, because he has such a saintly patience with fools, which must practically kill him as he's an incredibly intelligent man himself...'

CHAPTER FOUR

SISTER MARIE-PIERRE had brought her rosary beads but had not brought one or two other things which were important to her faith and prayer, so Isabelle was able to promise her that a phone call would be made to the convent and someone would bring them. This seemed to reassure the frail old nun and yet Isabelle thought she detected some remaining anxiety.

'Is there anything else you need?' she asked.

'No, no… But, tell me, when is it that I will be able to leave the hospital? By Wednesday, perhaps?'

'Oh, no, Soeur Marie-Pierre. The doctor will want you in for a week at least and probably longer, I should think, to make sure you're really well.'

'A week…' The news seemed to upset her, and Isabelle hastened to tell her that her condition had improved already. Her fever had fallen, as had her pulse and respiratory rates. But the aura of anxiety remained.

After lunch she received a visitor from the convent—Sister Cecile, who had brought the pictures of the Virgin and St Peter that Sister Marie-Pierre had asked for. Sister Cecile was, if anything, more frail in appearance than the tiny woman in the bed, and Sister Marie-Pierre's softly-lined and nutcracker-shaped face did not look any more cheerful at the other's report that, 'We're managing as much as we can without you.'

It was sunny and warm today after the late break in yesterday's rain, and as the afternoon warmed to its zenith the old nun kept staring out of the window. From where she lay, propped up in bed, she could see the dome of the original sixteenth-century hospital building, its age-greened copper roof giving off shimmering waves of heat.

By half past two she seemed so agitated at the sight that the visiting physiotherapist reported to Isabelle, 'I can't get her to concentrate so my pounding is doing very little because she won't cough sufficiently to finish the job!'

'What *is* it, Sister Marie-Pierre?' Isabelle said pleadingly, taking the papery hands in hers.

Their palms were calloused and work-worn, and it was easy to understand how illness had taken hold when the old woman pushed herself so hard. The physiotherapist had had to leave for her next patient, the session having been a disappointment.

The answer was unexpected. 'It's…it's my garden.'

'Your *garden?*'

'Yes, my vegetables. They are ripe and will be ripening more by the minute. My tomatoes, courgettes, *citrouilles*. With this weather they will not last more than a day or two before spoiling. And my lettuces and spinach will bolt to seed if they're not picked very soon.'

'Can we tell someone else to do it for you? Sister Cecile?'

'She does the cooking…and she is too frail for gardening.' Sister Marie-Pierre listed the other sisters of the little community on her fingers. Two more were too frail, another was also sick and the two youngest and strongest were away.

'Could I do it?' Isabelle suggested.

Then Jacques added behind her, 'With my help, Sister Marie-Pierre?'

Isabelle had not heard his approach and was startled, a reaction which quickly melted into frank pleasure at the sight of him in dark suit pants and a pale grey shirt.

'Would you?' A wrinkled hand darted out to caress his forearm and Sister Marie-Pierre crooned delightedly, 'Look, so big and strong. How wonderful you are, the two of you, to offer it. Both so young! You could do it in no time and feel no fatigue at all!'

Jacques laughed at her admiration of his strength. 'I'd be happy to.'

'And deliver them, too?' the nun continued eagerly at once.

'Deliver them?'

'I have a list. Poor families and old people living alone who are too frail to shop and do not eat as they should.' It didn't seem to occur to this selfless bride of Christ that she fitted this description as well. 'Fresh vegetables!' she went on. 'What could be more nourishing to make a good soup or a salad! Sister Cecile can direct you to the garden and tell you what to do.'

'It's settled, then, *ma soeur,*' Isabelle said, patting the old hand that was plucking restlessly now at the turned-back sheet. 'Dr Ransan and I will take care of it, and you are not to worry any more.'

'But when, Isabelle?' he said to her out in the corridor a minute later. 'I must be at the university in ten minutes to give my lecture, and it doesn't finish until five. That's late for you...'

'It doesn't matter. Couldn't you meet me there after your lecture? I'll go home first to change and have a snack and, if I get there a little before you, I don't mind starting alone.'

'You know where it is?'

'Yes, I had a long walk yesterday afternoon and came across it up on the hill there.'

'And...dinner afterwards?' He ran his fingers down her arm to meet and squeeze her hand briefly.

She felt his breath on her hair and the enveloping aura of his scent and warmth, and could have melted against

him then and there if this hadn't been far too public a place.
He was perfectly well aware of this response, what was
more, and sealed it with a searing kiss that trailed across
her lips for a second and then was over—to leave only a
throb of desire.

Isabelle floated through report, but managed to give a
coherent and accurate account of her patients' current
status. She couldn't help enjoying the times when Jacques's
name crossed her tongue. 'Dr Ransan has prescribed inhaled drug therapy to ease the constriction.' 'Dr Ransan
wants to be told at once if there's any deterioration.'

AT HOME, half an hour later, she changed into pipe-legged
jeans and a dark green cotton blouse that came loose to her
thighs, ate a *brioche aux raisins* and an apple and drank
some hot chocolate. Then she twisted her lively hair up
beneath an exotic scarf, which coiled like a gypsy's on the
back of her head, and set off up the hill along the Rue
Monceau, past the Église Saint-Paul and through to the
square where Vesanceau's Roman ruins basked in mossy
decay.

The clock struck a quarter past four and she sat for a
few minutes on a bench in a patch of sunshine. The big
church looked beautiful and she could see some stained
glass that would be magnificently rich and colourful from
the inside on such a bright day. Only somehow she didn't
feel quite morally pure enough to enter a church today,
despite the good deed she was on her way to perform in
the Order of Claire vegetable garden.

Her promise to Claire Oudot weighed more heavily on
her by the hour. It was like…like indigestion, and if *that*
wasn't a romantic comparison…! She could forget about it
for a time, then suddenly it would be burning her insides
again. She thought, If Jacques and I are going to keep finding reasons to see each other…and, oh, I want to, and I'm

sure he does, too! I told Claire 'for the time being', and
she probably thinks that means weeks or even months, but
this pretence has to end *soon*. I must talk to her about it,
and as soon as I have I'll tell Jacques.

It was the right decision, and it propelled her on up the
hill on lighter feet.

The Monastère Saint Claire was hidden behind a wall,
but the door in the wall was open so Isabelle entered the
paved courtyard and soon found Sister Cecile, who directed
her down a narrow stone passage to the sloping garden.
Walled in old grey stone, it was sunny, untidy and large
with magnificent views of the river Loque and the hills
beyond and contained a stone grotto dedicated to the
Virgin.

And it had vegetables! Sister Cecile had provided her
with sturdy plastic buckets, and she began at the bottom of
the garden, chasing the sun as it retreated slowly up the
slope. Lettuces and spinach first, shaking the rich soil from
the roots and resting each leafy green head carefully in the
buckets, then the round, golden pumpkins and the taut,
green-skinned courgettes.

Jacques arrived as she was tackling these, and she saw
him as she straightened, hefting a courgette that had been
overlooked beneath a canopy of rough-textured leaves during Sister Marie-Pierre's earlier harvests and was now as
big as a baby and almost as heavy.

He was casually dressed now too, in jeans and a white
T-shirt that emphasised the natural olive of his skin and
made it abundantly clear that, though his height and relaxed
stance brought the adjective 'lanky' to mind, there was
nothing gangling or under-developed about that very male
torso.

Looking into the sun, he squinted and shaded his eyes
with one hand so that she felt safe in watching him openly
as he negotiated the maze of damp, mossy paths between

the rather dilapidated garden beds to come down to her.
The problem was that she simply couldn't take her eyes off
him, and he'd reached her before she had a chance to take
that definitely besotted smile from her face.

The result was a happy one—he kissed her, first remov-
ing that impossibly huge courgette from her arms and then
lifting her to one of the raised beds with a muttered, 'Much
more convenient...'

Sister Marie-Pierre would have fretted badly if she could
have seen them. How would her vegetables ever get picked
and delivered when her strong young workers were standing there kissing in the late sunshine by the blowsy autumn
roses?

Perhaps it was partly the fault of those roses. They gave
lavishly of their scent and seemed to bless the moment with
it, making Isabelle aware of every sense as she stood in the
strong circle of Jacques's arms—tasting him, loving the feel
of the soft cotton T-shirt against her hands and the warmth
of his brown skin beneath.

It was after quite some time that he finally nuzzled her
face with his nose, traced a path of kisses along her jaw-
line and deliberately broke the mood with a murmured,
'You smell of lettuce, *petite* Isabelle, and of garden soil.'

She freed herself indignantly of his hold to retort, 'And
so would you, Dr Ransan, if you'd deigned to do any work!
I was suspicious of that pristine T-shirt as soon as I saw it,
but, let me tell you, it won't be pristine for much longer!'

Looking around for an appropriate weapon, she seized
handfuls of petals from the full-blown roses—pink and yellow and red and cream—pelting him with them until he
was laughing and cowering.

'Mercy! Please, Isabelle, have mercy!'

'Oh, pull yourself together. It's not doing a thing to
you...unfortunately!'

'Except giving me visions of making love to you in a sea of these cool, fragrant things. Feel!'

He gathered some now, too, took her in his arms again and lifted one hand to let the petals rain gently on both of them as they kissed once more. It ended in laughter again as a clinging beetle emerged with fussy affront from beneath a petal resting on Isabelle's shoulder and started off in search of firmer foundation and tastier food. Jacques scooped it up with one finger and it clung to the tip, near his well-shaped pink nail, until he successfully returned it to the roses.

'And now,' he said, 'since you've so thoroughly put me to shame...'

He began to pick the tomatoes while Isabelle finished the courgettes and tackled the beans—not very systematically, it had to be said, because she was so distracted by the way his body moved, leaning and bending, stretching and pulling. The way his jeans pulled taut across his well-muscled behind, the glimpse of brown skin at his waist where his shirt had come untucked, the shadowy suspicion of dark hair on his chest beneath the white cotton knit...

It was almost six by the time they finished, standing at the top of the now-shadowed garden with seven buckets of produce and one enormous courgette. Here thyme spilled over a low, dilapidated stone edging and it gave off its fragrance, crushed beneath their feet. In the same bed there were bountiful plantings of basil, parsley, sage and rosemary, and Isabelle said doubtfully, 'She didn't mention the herbs...'

'We could pick some of them, and if they're unwanted I'll take you to my place and make you an *omelette aux fines herbes*.'

'Let's pick lots of them, then, so we can't possibly give it all away...' she suggested brazenly, and his laugh was very warm.

It took them nearly two hours more to deliver their harvest to the addresses on the list that Sister Cecile gave them. At two or three places the people who came to the door of the ugly houses or tiny, featureless apartments were surly and ungrateful and Isabelle marvelled at the strength of Sister Marie-Pierre's commitment to such people, but everywhere else the fresh food was received with gratitude and people were very upset to hear that the old nun was ill in hospital.

'If my son comes,' one thin old man said, 'I'll ask him to take me to visit her, but he hasn't been for three weeks, so who can say? I can't get that far on my own these days. But I'll make a good soup tonight with all this... It'll last me for days.'

'Plenty of herbs left, Isabelle...' Jacques said lightly when they had finished.

'And I'm starving.'

So he did as he had promised, taking her in his blue Citroën back to his place—which turned out to be a charming apartment, reached through a tunnel-like entrance between the shop-fronts in the Rue du Pont which was scarcely wide enough for his car to pass through without scraping off the doorhandles.

A flight of stone steps, made bright by earthenware pots of red geraniums, led to a secluded interior where a masculine forest green and rust colour scheme and wood and leather furnishings were offset by cream floor rugs, curtains and paintwork. There was one large bedroom and a comfortable study that doubled as a guest-room, a gleaming white bathroom and the sort of kitchen where an *omelette aux fines herbes* seemed like snack food.

While Isabelle chopped the herbs—she had resisted his urging that she loll on that russet leather couch—he produced the long stick of bread they'd bought on their way home, set out cheeses on a platter, opened white wine and tossed a simple salad of lettuce, cress and endives. There was even an apple tart, also freshly purchased, and coffee to follow.

With candles lit and the wine just poured, the omelettes piping hot and perfectly shaped onto gold-rimmed cream plates, and cheese, dessert and coffee all in readiness, the stage was set—and perhaps what happened in the hours that followed was inevitable.

After that simple, delectable meal had been reduced to mere memory and after the complex ephemeral tapestry of a long conversation had been woven in the air, they slept together.

Isabelle had never done it before.

Well, yes, she had done '*it*' before, back in British Columbia, but then only after a lot of careful thought about the state of the relationship and her feelings for the fellow nurse, Brian. Even so, despite all that analysis the relationship hadn't lasted and she'd been left with a vague sense of having been misled, not by Brian—who was a decent enough guy—but by her own attempts to be sensible.

This time... *This* was what she had never done before. To plunge into the most physical of connections with a man so quickly—when she barely knew him, when *nothing* had been discussed and when she hadn't even thought about concepts of good sense or anything else.

It was madness. Sheer madness. Sheer, divine, fabulous madness...

That moment when he asked her, his voice husky with desire and his lips soft and lazy because they'd already been kissing on the couch for what seemed like hours, 'Isabelle, would you stay tonight?'

The moment after she said a tremulous, 'Yes,' when he didn't even wait for anything more but simply swept her up into his arms and carried her through to his bed with triumph and hunger and happiness radiating from every pore of him.

The many moments that followed—tumbling, sensuous, dark, too fluid to grasp in memory although somehow her body was able to relive them later and be bathed again in the vibrantly physical sensation of union.

His eyes didn't leave her face as he fluidly undressed her, then stripped away his own clothing. He didn't turn on the bedroom light but a lamp still glowed through from the sitting-room, creating a long, golden panel of light that made his long body look enormous in shadow.

It seemed incredible that he knew so well how to please her...although, when she used the same instinct to find the sources of his pleasure, it seemed the most natural and obvious thing in the world and she could only assume fuzzily that there was some unspoken connection that made this all possible.

Afterwards they both fell asleep almost at once, still fitted closely together, and she didn't wake until a soft, cool light began to seep very faintly into the room and an odd sense of bereftness told her that he was gone from the bed.

When she woke up for several minutes she felt terrible and didn't have a clue what she could be doing here in the bed of a man who was surely almost a stranger. Then he came in, freshly showered and dressed and smiling easily at her, and she mused, he's not a stranger. From the first moment I saw him he didn't feel like a stranger. Look at that smile. *He* doesn't regret it.

She smiled back at him, a little timidly, and he groaned. 'Don't say or do the slightest thing to invite me back into that bed with you, Isabelle. I must be at the hospital within an hour.'

'What time is it?'

'Not yet six. If you dress quickly I can drop you home. No time for breakfast.'

He left the room again and she scrambled into her clothes, not dashed or dampened, exactly, by the fact that things suddenly had to be practical but wishing it could be different all the same.

And it wasn't until he'd quietly pulled up in front of Claire's and scanned the elderly woman's still-shuttered windows doubtfully that the first real regret hit home. She had slept with him, and he still didn't know who she was. That alone was proof that it had happened too soon.

'She sleeps late, I think,' he said, still obviously thinking of Claire.

'Yes, I think so.'

'Our secret is safe a little longer, then. And now... I will see you, *petite* Isabelle, as soon as it can be arranged.'

'Within an hour or two at the hospital,' she reminded him, thinking about how hard it was going to be to act naturally.

'But I didn't mean *that*, of course...'

'No...'

'I meant...' He didn't finish the sentence with words, just with a brief kiss that brushed fiercely and crookedly across her mouth, leaving its imprint like a burn.

Then he sped away, to leave her thinking, our secret? What about *my* secret? That promise to Claire. I have to ask her to release me from it at once!

But Claire's apartment was quite silent as she tiptoed past it, and she remembered that the other woman had been going out last night and was probably sleeping in. Absently and without appetite, she drank coffee and ate a stale heel of yesterday's stick of bread smeared with butter. Then she got herself ready, all the while listening intently for any sound coming from below, but there was nothing and eventually, cutting it very fine, she had to leave.

Hurrying to the hospital along the crooked streets, she found herself hoping perversely that she wouldn't see

Jacques at all today because the fruitless wait for Claire had only made that promise and her need to be rid of it loom more urgently and ominously. By the time she reached the ward she was feeling desperately guilty and chafingly impatient to get through the day. As long as it was routine, as uneventful as possible…

It wasn't, of course.

Madame Chaillet's condition still remained a mystery and she was growing increasingly ill, receiving several different drugs to ease her alarmingly diverse symptoms but nothing to treat the underlying cause. Her course of wide-spectrum antibiotics was like shooting darts into a pitch-black room in the hope of hitting a bullseye. There was talk of sending her up to Intensive Care but Jacques had been resisting this, as if he felt that this would be admitting that she could well die.

She was still sleeping deeply—under the effects of her increasingly heavy medication—early in the morning when he came in to examine her once again, conferring with Remy Chapuis at the bedside while Isabelle took routine observations.

They were both incredibly aware of each other, Isabelle nervously so and Jacques happily. It should have made her happy, too, to see those open, helpless smiles he kept giving her whenever Dr Chapuis wasn't looking but, instead, her tension was winding tighter and tighter and she couldn't smile back at him in the same way at all.

The strength of her response to him was beginning to terrify her and might have done even without her family relationship to him and her promise to Claire. *With* those complications…

How could I have let it happen?

Jacques wasn't smiling any more. He'd noticed her ambivalence, then…

But, in fact, it was Madame Chaillet who was making him frown like this.

'I still favour tuberculosis,' Dr Chapuis was saying. 'It can present with these wide-ranging symptoms, and the chest X-ray—'

'The chest X-ray was wrong for TB,' Jacques answered firmly. 'And the bronchoscopy didn't indicate it either. We'll wait for the sputum cultures to rule it out completely, of course. Meanwhile, there's so much going on here that...well, unlikely as it may seem and though there's nothing in her history to suggest it...I want to test her for HIV. We can no longer afford to make *any* assumptions here!'

'*Nom de Dieu!* Do you think she has a bit of a night-time clientele on the side?' Remy Chapuis cracked coarsely.

Isabelle, unseen, rolled her eyes at Madame Chaillet's blood-pressure cuff and lost count of the pulse she was taking from the still-sleeping woman, while Jacques said in a voice of ominous quiet behind her, 'It would be as well if you learnt to resist these impulses for derogatory humour, Dr Chapuis. If we are going to make jokes at all, let us make them *to* the patient not *about* her. I did think I had made this point quite clear yesterday when we discussed Sister Marie-Pierre's case, but evidently I was not clear enough. For that...I apologise.' The irony was deadly.

'Oh, that's...quite all right, Doctor,' Remy Chapuis stammered.

'Have I expressed myself better this time?' Still his voice was not raised.

There was a strangled pause, then, 'Oh, yes, very clearly! I—'

'Good.' Fluidly he turned away from the younger doctor, leaving the man floundering, and said to Isabelle, 'She's stirring, I think, Mademoiselle Bonnet. Has she eaten breakfast yet?'

'No, she's somehow slept through all the ward's morning noise so we haven't brought it in yet. In any case, she has very little appetite, Dr Ransan. Those mouth and throat ulcers are troubling her.'

'And there's still evidence of gastro-intestinal bleeding?'

'I'm afraid so.'

He shook his head, then rubbed his temples with a large hand, reminding her that it was only a week since he'd been laid low with flu...the day they'd met. Surely it had to be longer ago than that? That hand of his was already so familiar, and had felt so *right* on her skin last night. She shuddered, a stomach-churning mixture of intense sensual memory and fearful regret flooding her.

'I'm going to look through all those test results again,' Dr Chapuis was saying industriously. 'With the insufficiency of her adrenal gland function and the low platelet count, I'm wondering...' He bustled off but, if he was expecting this show of dedication and competence to impress his senior, he would have been disappointed at Dr Ransan's expression...because it wasn't directed anywhere near him, nor was it focused on Madame Chaillet, who was looking listlessly and groggily up at Jacques now.

'Not enough sleep,' Jacques said with a teasing smile. 'I must learn not to invite guests over in the middle of the week...although I suspect I may want to even more in the future.'

'I— Yes,' she blurted awkwardly. 'I want to, Jacques, but—'

It didn't make any sense at all, and his impatient frown was hardly surprising. There was an uncomfortable moment of silence, then he said, 'Look, Isabelle, could you come into the corridor for a moment?'

This time his gaze didn't fully meet her own, and Isabelle's heart began to beat faster. Clearly he had detected her awkwardness, and she realised that she should have tried harder to conceal it because there was no explanation for it that she was free to give yet. All she had done was to take that glowing, wonderful happiness from his face, and it made the breath catch in her throat to think that he'd felt that way about their night.

I should be over the moon as well if he's feeling so strongly. I was. I *would* have been... He's not going to demand an explanation *now,* is he?

Looking up at him, she saw the sudden weariness sketched in the lines of his tall body and a tautness to his mouth that she longed to kiss away.

'Did—did you want...?' she began awkwardly, now that they were alone outside the patient's room.

'Madame Chaillet's illness,' he said.

And she realised at once, Of course! He's far too professional to want to thrash out our response to each other in the middle of the ward when there's this patient so dangerously ill and we don't know what's going on.

'There's something we're missing,' he said crisply. 'I want you to think about every single thing she said to you last week before she got so bad. Not just what she gave in answer to our questions but her general conversation. There has to be a clue for us, surely!'

'I—I don't know.' She had to grope to get her thoughts back on track. 'Even last week she was feeling pretty rotten. She didn't talk much. Just about how annoying this was.'

'She still thought of it in those terms? As something of a nuisance? She's a stoic!'

'Yes, she said she'd been fit as a fiddle over the summer,' Isabelle recollected, her focusing firming in the right place now. 'Her asthma was well controlled, she felt she'd recovered quickly from the flu bout and she'd even done some work around the farmyard for her son. She couldn't understand how one day she could be forking hay, mucking out the pigsty and tearing down the old poultry roost and a few days later "this relapse of the flu", as she was calling it at first, was knocking her flat. Perhaps it wasn't flu in the first place, as she thought, though. Perhaps—'

But Jacques's fists had balled and he was smacking them together in satisfaction. 'That's it! At last! Histoplasmosis! The fungus was released into the air when she shook out all those ancient bird droppings! It's got to be!' Now he swore, and the momentary triumph was gone. 'And we've let it go unrecognised and untreated for a week. Damnation! If only I hadn't been sick myself! We must take her off those antibiotics at once because they're doing nothing for her.'

He turned on his heel without further explanation and strode away, to leave her whole body immediately bereft as he called, 'Dr Chapuis? Where have you got to?'

They met up outside the door of the next four-bed room while Isabelle was still staring helplessly after him. 'Disseminated histoplasmosis!' he told the junior doctor. 'We'll culture it, but I'm positive it has to be. With her immune system compromised from the steroids she takes for her asthma and from the recent bout of flu she mentioned, I suspect the disease didn't resolve itself as it would have done in someone younger and fitter. So now we've got this far more serious dissemination of the fungus.'

'To be treated with…?'

'One of the nastiest drugs in the modern pharmacopoeia,' he finished on a steely sigh.

Half an hour later he told Isabelle at the nurses' station, 'There's no choice, I'm afraid.'

He leaned over her—she was at a desk, writing notes—so that his white coat gaped open to show the pale green shirt beneath.

'With the drug?' she asked.

'Yes, it's a particularly notorious anti-fungal agent, but with the extent of this disease's spread—and I've been racking myself but we can't be blamed for not picking it up earlier because its manifestations are so diverse—she'll die if we don't use it.'

'No...!'

'She may die if we do because this stuff can bring on kidney failure, and even its more benign side-effects are unpleasant. Which is why I'm setting this drip up myself initially, using the strictly aseptic technique that we're all supposed to use and most of us are sloppy about at times. And it's why I want you to stay with Madame Chaillet for the next few hours while we gradually step up the rate of infusion.'

She swivelled to face him, and he straightened and began to pace as she asked, 'What should I be looking for?'

'In these first critical hours? Fever, chills, shaking, hypotension, anorexia...'

'Oh, no! Poor Madame Chaillet! After all she's going through already!'

'And,' he continued inexorably, 'nausea, vomiting, headache and rapid breathing.'

'And she has to be on this for...?'

'Ten weeks. But the severity of those side-effects tapers off. If she can get through these first few days... Then, of course, we have to start monitoring her kidney function. And don't let anyone use this drip site to take blood or administer any other drugs. We don't want to play around with it.'

'Sterile dressing, changed every day?'

'Yes, please!'

He began to set up the drip, with Isabelle at his side to reassure Madame Chaillet who was now awake and alert.

Apprehensive, too, now that she had been told of her diagnosis.

'I knew there was something you could get from chicken droppings,' she said, 'but doesn't it just go away?'

Jacques explained about the way her necessary steroid use had compromised her immune system and gave as honest an account as he could of what they expected to happen now. There was no sense in upsetting her…and yet she had to know the options that were being weighed.

'So I have three choices,' she summarised. 'Let this disease finish me off, let that drug finish me off…or fight both of them!'

'Look at it that way and you should do all right,' Jacques said, chafing her shoulder with rough concern.

'Get on with it, then, Doctor, please!'

He began the infusion very slowly, adjusting the rate so that the drug would take several hours to flow into Madame Chaillet's veins. 'I may step up the rate in two hours,' he told Isabelle, 'so I'll want your report then on any symptoms. Let's see, it's eight now. Start looking for those reactions in about an hour, and I'll be back at ten.'

He left, and because the nurses' station was crowded there was nothing in the brief flash of his smile but the courtesy of a doctor to a nurse. It was frightening. If last night was a one-night stand—oh, I've been crazy—then in a few days nothing might be left of it at all. Have I been a complete fool?

Back at ten, he had said, but in fact he returned before that. One of his cystic fibrosis patients had come in to await a possible heart-lung transplant, and he needed to assess her status and stand by for the surgery, should it take place.

He glanced in at Isabelle and Madame Chaillet and mouthed a brief, *'Ça va?'*

She nodded. *'Ça va.'* It's fine.

There was no sign yet of the side-effects he was ex-

pecting from the drug. It was barely nine, and the drip still
ran with a maddening slowness. At times it was hard not
to watch it, holding her breath as the clear liquid swelled,
trembled for an instant and then fell into the tube that
snaked, transparent, to Yvette Chaillet's motionless hand.
The elderly woman was lying with closed eyes, too ill to
speak.

After this, Isabelle saw Jacques prowling outside between the nurses' station and his CF patient's room, using
the phone several times and then consulting with the transplant surgeon and his team who had come to see the patient.

Then suddenly the surgical team left and all was quiet
again…except that now Madame Chaillet's reactions had
started and her thorough but uncomplaining misery com-
manded Isabelle's full attention.

When Jacques appeared as promised at ten she steeled
herself to ask him quietly, 'What's happening with the
transplant?' and saw his face twist with disappointment.

'The donor's family changed their minds about consent.
It happens. And it's…not productive…to feel angry with
people who are dealing with a very fresh bereavement.
Unfortunately it's happened twice to Michelle now, and
she's losing hope. She's pretty sick. I'm going to keep her
in for a while to try and get her a bit stronger so we can
hang on until her next chance.' He turned towards the bed.
'Meanwhile, Madame Chaillet, *ma chère*…'

'Don't ask her to talk,' Isabelle came in quickly, and
summarised the past half-hour's nausea, chills and increas-
ing fever. 'Her blood pressure is dropping, too, as you said
it might.'

'I won't increase the infusion rate yet, then,' he said, and
added in a low voice, 'But what about you, Isabelle? Can
I ask *you* to talk? Things are so hectic today, but after last
night… You don't seem happy. Surely you're not sorry
about such a beautiful time?'

He touched the warmth of her neck with a light, caressing stroke and she could so easily have leant against his hand and stayed there. Instead, she just made herself wait until his fingers had gone again.

'We will talk,' she promised him awkwardly, not able to meet his searching gaze. 'We will, Jacques, as soon as I... Well, soon.'

He nodded, still frowning, but said only, 'I'll be back in two hours to check this drip again.'

He was, and then again at two. At three she handed over to a very competent nurse of about her own age who clucked and winced when she heard of Madame Chaillet's diagnosis and treatment. 'Poor thing!'

'The reaction is tapering off now.'

'And the others?'

'Doing well. Sister Marie-Pierre is feeling a little better, she says, though I'm not quite convinced. In any case, she never gives a bit of trouble. Madame Guinchard will be discharged on Thursday, we think. It's this one you'll be working with today...'

They both looked towards Madame Chaillet, who lay with her eyes closed, sweating and trembling and taking rapid, shallow gasps of air. In addition to the antifungal drug she was receiving her usual asthma medication, as well as something to prevent the stress ulcers that could be caused by steroid use and two more drugs to treat her symptoms of nausea and fever. Isabelle murmured a brief farewell to the sick woman, but there was just a brief fluttering of her eyelids and a pale, flat smile in reply.

Shaking off the mood of the ward, Isabelle turned her attention to her own concerns and set off at a rapid pace for home—skirting milling groups of students who had just spilled from lectures at the nearby university. There were some comments from one or two of the men, well meant enough to coax a smile from her, and the students were good-looking in a way she would have drooled over at eighteen.

But they seem too *unfinished* these days, she thought. Cocky and confident, even though they haven't actually proved themselves very much at all. Compared to Jacques...

'May I buy you coffee, *Mademoiselle Infirmière?*' a third student suggested.

'Sorry, but I only drink milk,' Isabelle answered lightly, and hurried on before she was further ensnared. She needed to see Claire *now!*

CHAPTER FIVE

'COME in, my dear. I've just put some coffee on, hoping you would pay me a visit.' She caught sight of Isabelle's fraught expression. 'Or would you prefer chocolate?'

'Oh, it doesn't matter,' Isabelle answered distractedly. 'Coffee is fine.' She followed Claire into the kitchen. 'I need you to release me from that promise I made to you. It's time to tell Jacques who I am, Madame Claire!'

The coffee-cup clattered in the elderly woman's hand, but she asked in a steady voice, 'What has happened to make you feel this so strongly?'

'I... We...'

'You don't have to say it. There's an attraction between you. I saw it the other night when we brought poor Jeanne to the hospital.'

'Yes...all right. Only now he has no idea what's going on. I hate not being honest so I was behaving *very* strangely to him today, Claire, and not surprisingly... Pouf! What you saw the other night may already have gone up in smoke, so *please*...!' She couldn't bring last night into it, feeling so frightened and foolish about having let it happen.

'Oh, my dear, no!' Claire abandoned the coffee preparations and turned to Isabelle, seizing supple nurse's hands with her own ringed fingers and squeezing them almost painfully. 'How can I convince you that if you are attracted to him that is all the more reason to keep silent?'

'*How* can you convince me?' Isabelle echoed, angry and agitated as she shook off the demanding grip. 'You can't!

Or rather, there's only one possible way and that's by telling me the whole truth, Madame Claire.'

'The *whole* truth?'

'I'm far from stupid. I could almost *feel* the past in the air between you and Cousin Jeanne the other night, like—like cobwebs clinging to both of you. You seem to be as closely bound up with the Ransan family as if you were part of it, and yet you're not. I've seen how much you care about Jeanne and Jacques. Who are you? What *were* you to the Ransan family?'

Claire sighed. 'Why, your great-uncle's mistress, of course. I thought your mother might have told you *that*.'

There was something very incongruous about the little scene ten minutes later. Claire had insisted on preparing and serving the coffee and cakes, as well as a healthy chunk of bread and cheese for Isabelle who munched absently, listening to Claire's story and trying to get her woolly wits around the facts.

Charles Ransan's mistress.

'It began in 1945, when I was twenty-one and he was ten years older,' Claire said. 'He was away for most of the war, fighting with the Resistance. He was quite a hero, but that didn't make him a kinder man. He valued perfection—physical and mental—too highly. And when he got home and saw how much worse Jeanne's back had become—she was seven by then—he decreed that there should be no more children. Marie, his wife, had had three miscarriages as well, and he felt that her womb must be tainted.'

'*What?*'

'That was an old-fashioned idea, I know, but it was the way people often thought then. Marie was devout and would not practise birth control so their marital relations ceased. He had needs, and I... Well, I made a good mistress.' There was the faintest of smiles.

'Oh, I'm...sure you did!'

'It lasted until 1958, but then I ended it. I'd become so fond of the children, you see, François and Jeanne—and Berenice, your mother, who was Jeanne's friend and soon to become engaged to François—and I knew that their father was not making them happy. He pushed François too hard and refused to see any promise at all in Jeanne. His disgust at her deformity was very evident and he humiliated her constantly about her ambitions as a designer. I thought that perhaps if he stopped seeing me he might pay more attention to his children and come to value and understand them better.'

'And did he?'

'No, in fact it got worse. But by then I was in love with another man, the one who bought me this house…and who objected so strongly to my smoking in it! We were together for twenty-eight years until his death, and since then I have been alone.'

'You were married?'

'No, my dear!' She gave a reluctant laugh. '*He* was, but not to me!'

'And Marie Ransan and this other man's wife—they knew about you?'

'Ah, no! I took very great care that they should not! No… To be honest, Marie might have suspected because of the interest I took in Jeanne and François, but I'm quite certain that Adelie Beliard never did. She was a nasty woman, and cared for her eight dogs far more than she did for her three children!'

Claire's memories had distracted her for a few moments from the matter at hand, but now she focused sharply on Isabelle once again. 'So you see, Isabelle, now that I've told you everything just how it is that I know the value of secrecy in affairs of the heart?'

This brought Isabelle back into full control of her faculties. 'That's completely different from my situation,' she responded spiritedly. 'And you *haven't* told me everything! About yourself, yes, but not about Cousin François and my mother...and Jacques. You've told me why you know it, but not what you know and you must see that I need to hear it, Madame Claire!'

Her hands were clasped quite beseechingly now.

'Oh, my dear, all you need to know is this. It's not the broken engagement that Jacques can't forgive your parents for. It's a matter of money.'

'Money?'

'He thinks your father... Well, he feels he lost out financially. It's not important, and the details are...' She waved vaguely. 'But to most Frenchmen, as to most people everywhere, I imagine, a dispute over money can be far more bitter than one over that dubious commodity known as love! And you disagree with me completely, and that's delightful!'

Isabelle glared, then rose and paced, her coffee cooling and her cake untouched.

Claire sighed.

'Tell him,' she said quietly, 'because I can see you will have no peace until you do. It will ruin things between you but if, as you say, your unwilling silence is ruining them anyway...' She sighed again. 'It is a pity because it was a delightful idea that the two of you should come together, but perhaps it was impossible all along.'

THE BRASS PLATE that read JACQUES RANSAN, PNEUMOLOGUE in engraved black letters gleamed to a degree that suggested daily polishing. It was arranged with several others at eye level on the stone façade of an old building, whose huge and elaborately carved outer door opened into an archway leading to a cobbled courtyard. Crossing this courtyard at about five o'clock, having left Claire's with indecent haste, Isabelle entered another archway and there were Jacques's name and professional title again on a door to the left.

She had agonised over whether to visit him at once in his professional rooms like this, but in the end it had seemed like the best choice as well as the one that strained her patience least. Far more private than the hospital, far less personal than his apartment…as long as she was permitted to see him.

That she might *not* be was a fact communicated to her at once, as he had apparently chosen a mechanical dragon rather than a human being to guard the sanctity of his suite. The dragon, complete with blood-red talons, uncurled itself from a loving inspection of its filing cabinets and said without preamble, 'You haven't got an appointment.'

'I— How did you know?'

'He's with his last patient of the day already.' There was a triumphant glare—not a fully *human* expression, it seemed to Isabelle, confirming her suspicion that she was definitely not dealing with the usual species of nurse-receptionist here.

Still, she tried to seize the advantage. 'However, since this is a personal matter an appointment isn't necessary.'

'On the contrary.' The dragon's smile defied description. 'An appointment is all the more necessary in such circumstances. I can't have the doctor bothered by these sorts of unscheduled interruptions. He would never get any work done!'

'You mean, women…? I mean, *people*…often come to see him for personal reasons without an appointment?' Isabelle queried rather bleakly.

'He has some very silly students,' was the cryptic response.

'I'm not a student.'

'Which gives you even less excuse.' She waited, silent, glaring again.

'Perhaps I'll just wait until he comes out, then,' Isabelle said after a moment, with more firmness than she felt internally.

You can tell a man by the company he keeps. Did whoever said that include receptionists?

'He usually exits via the rear door,' was the bone-chilling response.

Today, though, he didn't. Isabelle was on the point of admitting defeat, when an elderly man, wheeling portable oxygen equipment, came out of the door on the far side of the waiting-room, trundled past the dragon's lair—it was cunningly disguised as a desk—and exited with an apologetic wheeze which seemed to suggest a fear that the dragon would think he had designs on her treasured files.

A moment later there were some sounds from behind the far door and then Jacques himself appeared. 'Madame Trimaille, could you possibly—? Isabelle!' His face lit up and Isabelle's heart turned over.

'Am I to add her to the list, then, Dr Ransan?'

'Er, yes, please do, Madame Trimaille. Isabelle Bonnet.'

'I'm sorry, it seems I shouldn't have come without an appointment,' she said.

'No, no.' He waved absently at the desk and its denizen. 'Madame Trimaille has it all in hand. There's a list of people whom I'm allowed to have—that is to say, whom we will allow to wait without an appointment until she can buzz me. It's a system that…er…seems to work.' He winked and grinned.

'You had a question for me, Doctor?' Madame Trimaille came in.

'A couple of files. Doesn't matter now. You may leave for the day.'

'I will first finish the—'

'In fact,' he interrupted, suddenly very firm, 'I would *prefer* that you leave for the day, Madame Trimaille.'

'Yes, Doctor.'

'Come through, Isabelle.'

She followed him with alacrity.

'Whew!' Closing the waiting room door behind him, he muttered, 'I'm totally at her mercy. Could you tell?'

'No! I thought you seemed very much in control,' she told him sincerely. 'I was quite stunningly impressed.'

'What do you think she's made of? I've theorised that it's some kind of metallic alloy... I'm glad you've come, Isabelle.'

'I *had* to!'

His arm, warm and heavy, drawing her against him, felt for the moment like all the reassurance she really needed. She sank with willing relief into his arms, sure that it was going to be all right—laughing at herself for her fear and doubt today, already thinking again of his bed and their two selves in it.

'Good...' he said. 'Lovely Isabelle...'

'But why do you keep her on, then?' See, she was even relaxed enough to chat. 'Your dragon, I mean.'

He didn't bat an eyelid at her reference. 'She's a friend of my mother's, and she's as efficient as a machine. She *is* a machine!'

'What, a guillotine?'

'Something like that,' he agreed gloomily. 'She's certainly never been sick in the three years I've had her.'

'I almost left, actually. You came out just in time.'

'You're on the list now. She insisted on a list! It won't be a problem again. But now, *petite* Isabelle...' He swept her into his office. 'Why did you look so guilty and unhappy this morning? You've come to tell me, haven't you?'

'Yes...'

'First, just in case, may I kiss you?'

'Oh, please do...!'

It lasted a nice long time, well after the sound of keys

rattling, a door closing and sensible heels on the cobbles outside told them that Madame Trimaille had left for the day.

He took his glasses off and let them clatter onto his desk, then swept her up there too so that she could sit and he could stand and they could reach each other's lips without all that bending and stretching.

His lips... They were smooth and firm and delicious as he held her jaw lightly between his hands, then ran fluting fingers down her throat to brush at her breasts through the skimpy pink cotton top she had changed into after work. She hadn't been aware until now just how closely the cotton knit moulded itself against her figure...or was it just his hands, setting her skin on fire? There was an inch or two of bare midriff, as well, between the top and her jeans and his touch there tickled and sensitised her nerve endings into a frenzy of awareness.

'Do you know, you make me *hungry,* Isabelle,' he groaned against her mouth. 'I keep imagining that you are something delectable to eat. Your breasts are like little cups of *crème brûlée,* and your hair is like fresh *brioche.* I can see myself pooling chocolate onto that warm stomach and licking it off...'

She arched back and shuddered as he lifted her skimpy top to just below her breasts and buried his face in the flesh he had exposed. Her hands came convulsively to grip his head and tangle amongst the rich syrupy brown strands of his hair.

'Take off your jacket,' she urged huskily. 'I love it! You look so formal and serious in these suits you wear, and you're not formal *or* serious at all, which is so...so *nice,* and I feel like it's my secret about you... But take it off. I want to touch you more closely. Touch *you!*'

Impatiently she slid the dark jacket from his shoulders and massaged the hard rounded forms of his muscles as he let the garment slip unheeded from his arms and onto the floor. Then he stood back a little, grinning lazily as she explored him with her hands, and when he began to undo the buttons of his cream shirt she didn't try to stop him and swooped in to part the fabric as soon as it was free.

His chest was magnificent, naturally olive, its contours quite unblurred by fat. The pattern of black hair between his small, tight nipples was quite fine and compact, leaving the rest of his skin utterly smooth apart from one more fine dark line of hair that began just above his waist and arrowed down to his belted trousers, beyond which it…thickened invitingly.

But this wanton exploration and hungry imagining was bringing her to a level of dangerous abandonment, and she felt a moment of doubt as a thought occurred to her. I've only promised to be honest with him. That's in the air between us, making this possible, but the honesty hasn't actually *happened* yet…

She was on the point of pulling away, and her hands had stiffened and stilled against his chest, but then he groaned and his nipples tightened still more as he pulled her against him once again then slid his hands swiftly up to peel back that defenceless little pink top so that it bunched above her white lace bra and gave his lips full access to the slight, creamy shapes of her breasts.

'Yes,' he said, his face buried in the tender, achingly sensitive valley. 'Vanilla and caramel. *Crème brûlée.*'

'Jacques…'

'Do you know the scenarios I had today about what was wrong? You'll laugh if I tell you…so I will because I know you like to laugh and I love to hear it. Such a golden sound! She's married, I thought. She has a husband in British Columbia. Maybe two husbands! And she's lied about her age. She's not twenty-six at all, she's seventeen. Perhaps she's never been to British Columbia. That accent is faked, and she's from some back street in Paris and has men all over France whom she milks mercilessly.'

'Oh, Jacques! Nothing nearly so terrible as that!'

'Not even one husband?'

'Never! Nor am I engaged.'

'I'm actually disappointed, I think.'

'You will be...I hope,' she whispered, blessing him for the foolishness of it all because it seemed positively easy now to say it as she pillowed her ear against his chest. 'There's no real drama or scandal. I'm your second cousin, that's all, daughter of your father's cousin Raoul.'

There was a strangled exclamation, but she did not fully take this in and ran on happily, 'Yes, that dastardly man who ran off to Quebec with your father's fiancée. Madame Claire swore me to secrecy at first—there's something about money, too, apparently—but after thirty-five years it's so ridiculous, don't you think? I came here hoping that the next generation—you and I—could bridge the gap, and now it seems we're doing it in a better way than—'

'*Nom de Dieu*. Isabelle, will you stop?' he seethed.

Isabelle's quickened in-breath hissed between her teeth. He'd stiffened...horribly! *When*? She hadn't noticed, had gone bubbling on, so certain had she been that he wouldn't mind—that he'd think the family quarrel as petty and pointless as she did—but from his expression...

He rounded on his heel so that she couldn't see his face now, but every stark line of his body told her what she'd find in those brown eyes and that firm mouth if she moved from the desk to look.

The cream shirt lay half off one shoulder and he gave a flick of a shrug to cover the taut, smooth knob of bone and muscle once more, reminding her of the fact that her own torso, including half her breasts, was still exposed by the cotton top pleated now beneath her armpits.

She dragged it down to cover herself once more, too tense to breathe. 'Jacques…?'

'Raoul Bonnet's daughter. So you've just been playing at Romeo and Juliet, have you, with all this? This pretty seduction. Your willingness last night. You've known all along who I was. No wonder your response was so very—' His breath was a tightly controlled shudder. 'It was all a game for you.'

'No, Jacques! No! Is that why you're angry? It was real. My response to you was…*is*…real. The most wonderful, unexpected bonus.'

'Not any more.' There was a total finality to the words. 'What?'

'Not any more. It's not happening again, Isabelle. It can't. Not now.'

His face had hardened like molten steel setting in a mould, and suddenly she was as angry as he was.

'You mean I've *given* myself to you just for one night— a one-night stand?' she cried. 'I guess that makes it pretty easy for you to drop me, doesn't it? You got what you wanted, and now here's an easy excuse. Well, perhaps you didn't realise this but sleeping with someone is *not* something I do at the drop of a hat—'

'Oh, I realised it,' he muttered darkly, and this only made her angrier.

'Oh, you did, did you?' She was like a firecracker going off, sputtering, hot and loud in all directions at once, accusing him wildly because it *hurt* so much. 'You could tell? That's it, then, I suppose? I wasn't very good at it, or something, and you've decided you can't be bothered again.'

'God, *no*, Isabelle,' he thundered. 'Stop this!'

He seized her head in his hands, then dropped them away and buried his face in his large palms. 'This is *terrible!*'

'Yes, it is, isn't it?' She was close to tears now. 'So will you damn well tell me what's going on? *Why?* Claire said you'd react badly. She made me promise to bide my time before I told you.' The irony of it struck her. 'And I didn't believe her.'

'You should have, then,' Jacques responded heavily. 'My grandfather's mistress is surely in a position to know.'

'You know about that?'

'Of course.' He shrugged. 'I think most people do. I wasn't sure if you did.'

'Then you were hoping to shock me?' she challenged.

'Yes, Isabelle,' he answered heavily.

'Then tell me, Jacques Ransan, just what is so terrible about my father stealing your father's fiancée?'

He looked at her for a long moment. 'Nothing. If that was all he had stolen. I see that dear Madame Claire has been practising her usual selective truth-telling again, thinking she knows best.'

'You were suggesting just a minute ago that she did,' Isabelle managed to retort.

She was angry with Jacques...*furious*...and still bewildered but, beyond all this, what was that she could see in Jacques's face? A bitter, impotent and deeply-rooted hurt. She went on quietly, 'If there's more to the story, Jacques, then will you damn well tell it to me so that we can both stop making mountains out of molehills and perhaps—?'

He shook his head. 'It's easy enough to tell. I doubt that telling will make a difference. Your father stole some money from my grandfather then left for Canada, taking my father's fiancé with him and leaving *Papa* to receive the blame for the theft. My grandfather was...not a forgiving man—perhaps I've inherited a little of that trait!'

'I'm getting that impression...'

'He was convinced that my father was the thief and refused to have anything more to do with him. This included, of course, refusing to finance his medical studies any further. *Papa* tried to continue on his own but he'd married my mother by this time, and I was soon on the way and then my sisters two and four years later. He couldn't afford it and turned to managing the cheese shop where he still works today.

'Not quite what he'd dreamed of! And though I don't *condone* the fact that he drinks at times because of it, and makes my mother's life miserable when he does—they've never been happy together—I understand how thwarted ambition can have that effect. If I had been unable to study medicine—which I could only do because of the huge sacrifices my parents made for my sisters and myself—I can't predict what a shell of a man I might have become.'

Isabelle closed her eyes. 'Oh, Jacques...'

'Do you understand a little better now, perhaps?' The anger in his tone had softened, but only to be replaced by a tightly reined bitterness.

She said gropingly as she searched his face, 'I understand how difficult it must all have been.' Then with a bite of her own, 'I *don't* understand why you simply take it as read that my father is a thief! When Claire mentioned money I— Well, I didn't really think about what she might have meant. My father is *not* a thief! And if he *had* stolen any money he and my mother would have had an easier time of it establishing themselves in Canada. Those years before I was born were a struggle!'

'And if *my* father had stolen the money, then continuing his medical studies would have presented no problem,' Jacques came in bluntly. 'So what do you suggest actually happened?'

'I have absolutely no idea since this is the first I've heard of the whole story,' she pointed out. 'But, Jacques...' She had taken a deep breath, groping for what was really important here. 'Jacques?'

'Yes, Isabelle?'

He looked strained and wary, and for a moment she

didn't even know why she was trying. Why not just jump on the family bandwagon, storm off in a huff and perpetuate the feud for another generation until it attained the proportions of a medieval Scottish clan war?

Was it the lofty sentiments embodied in her initial peacemaking goal? Or simply the atavistic frenzy of her hormones because, angry or not, she couldn't even glance at this second cousin of hers any more without catching fire.

Maybe her reasons didn't matter.

'Since we don't know,' she suggested, weighing her argument even as she made it, 'well, we could argue about it for ever, I suppose, but wouldn't it be better to consign it to the past? Perhaps your grandfather was losing his marbles and never had this money in the first place. Perhaps the maid took it. Or a gang of mice chewed it up and made it into a nest.'

'Or it was taken by aliens in a spaceship,' he suggested drily, 'as evidence of the perverted priorities of Earthlings.'

'What a perfect solution!' she agreed with an edge. 'That way *no* one can be blamed, even for carelessness in leaving it in that coffee-can on the kitchen mantelpiece, or whatever the story might be. The point is—'

'I know what the point is, Isabelle,' he told her on a harsh sigh. 'I'm not a fool. It *is* Romeo and Juliet that you are suggesting.'

She saw the unmistakable flash of desire in those brown eyes as they raked over her, and felt a hot wash of relief and hope.

Then the desire was quenched by something much bleaker and he continued, 'But I can't do it. I've lived with my father's bitterness for too long; been caught in the middle of my parents' difficult dealings with one another. I can't bring you to them and calmly announce, "This is Isabelle, daughter of Raoul Bonnet, whom you have hated and blamed for thirty-five years, and I have fallen in love with her.'''

Those last words came out with a rawness which would have melted her completely if he had meant them in the here and now. 'So it must be nipped in the bud while that is still possible. It should still be possible. We have only known each other...' he shook his head and smiled briefly, then his eyes narrowed as though this calculation was more difficult than it should have been '...a little over a week.' He muttered something under his breath that she didn't catch.

'Are you saying that after much longer it...might *not* be possible?' she blurted breathlessly.

He spread his large hands and answered very simply, 'Yes!'

'Oh, heavens, you really are thinking like Romeo and Juliet!'

'Who were very young and very impetuous and, if Shakespeare will forgive me for this, very *selfish* people!' he retorted cuttingly. 'So there the comparison stops, I hope! There is to be no re-enactment of the fictional past here in Vesanceau. I simply will not do it to my father, no matter what the cost, when...*life,* let us say, has already betrayed him in so many other ways.'

The room was very silent now. Isabelle took in some of its details for the first time. The dark walnut bookcases filled with medical tomes, which flanked a large fireplace set with a mass of bronze, golden and rust-coloured chrysanthemums that mimicked the warmth of flames. The matching walnut desk. The padded leather chairs. The paintings on the walls—quietly beautiful oils, though no famous signatures adorned their corners.

And through that door to her right, she guessed, would be his examining rooms with an X-ray machine and possibly a bronchoscope as well. With his visiting rights at the prestigious Hôpital Saint-Jean and his lectureship in the medical faculty of the nearby university, his career was a very obvious success.

She said at last, rather abruptly, 'Doing as well as you are, couldn't you help your father in some way? Surely it's not to late for…for…'

'He won't let me. In any case, I'm still rather more beholden to the bank than I would like! But my father would not take a franc of my money. He is constantly urging me to establish myself securely, to pay off my debt…and to marry well.'

'Right,' she said tightly. 'And Raoul Bonnet's daughter or not, as a nurse I'd scarcely fall into that category!'

This admittedly wild accusation he would not accept, however. He had been standing some distance from her, restless on his feet and staring frequently and unseeingly at that warm glow of flowers in the fireplace, while she had slid off the desk some time ago and stood with its hard edges pressed into the softness of her upper thighs. Now he lunged towards her, seizing her arms with his powerful hands in a painful grip.

'You do *not* mean that, Isabelle! I will not have you leaving here today with that idea. Do you really think I would cold-bloodedly decide to marry well and then exclude you from consideration simply because—?'

He swore and then his mouth swooped onto hers to pluck greedily and desperately at her lips. 'I've told you what it is that has to keep us apart,' he said, still grazing her mouth.

'Then…then stop kissing me! Now!' she managed, although to have this continue would have been fiery delight.

He groaned. 'Yes! I'm sorry! I don't know what I'm saying or doing. I'm angry. Not at you—'

'You were!'

'Yes, I was. It was a shock. God, don't you understand that?'

'Your response has been a shock,' she muttered.

'I'm angry at the horrible irony of all this.' He laughed. 'I'm even angry at myself that I'm *not* Romeo—to cast family feeling to the four winds. Perhaps I've misjudged the boy.'

'Boy?'

'Romeo was a boy! I'm a man, Isabelle.' And he was, every inch of him, as her very female body was telling her even now all too clearly. 'A mature man, aware of the debt I owe to those who conceived and raised me. I will *not* pain my father by bringing you into his life!'

There was no doubt that he meant it. The strength of his will was equal to that of his long body. Numbly Isabelle realised that she had to go. Staying here alone with him like this, their response to each other heightened by too many conflicting, complex emotions, was far too danger-ous.

Am I as strong as he is? she wondered. Not physically, of course. As before, his height made her aware of her own petite, curved build in a way that had seemed deliciously sensual until now. But my will…my emotions. I understand how he feels. Trying to put myself in his place…yes. I'd agree. So I have to show him that. That we can be civilised about this, perhaps?

'I guess I'd better cancel that order I put in for a milking stool from the Dairymaid Emporium, then?' she made her-self say, and though they both laughed it wasn't a sunny sound.

'Are you going?' he asked quietly.

'Yes. What else is there to do?'

'Nothing else,' he agreed. 'I'm glad, though, that we've at least managed this so we're not enemies.'

'I'm not used to having enemies, Jacques, and I certainly don't intend to start with you.'

He was still staring at the flowers in the fireplace when she let herself carefully out of his office, and he didn't try to hold her back.

CHAPTER SIX

'WHAT'S going on down the corridor?' Dr Maryse Lefevre asked Isabelle, looking up from the chart she was studying as she stood near the window of this two-bed room.

The sophisticated blonde was a resident training in gastroenterology, and two of the patients in Isabelle's care today were here with gastric problems. It made a change...and meant that if she *did* see Jacques it was only a quick glimpse as he strode past an open door or paused briefly at the nurses' station to write up some notes.

Sister Boucher had instituted this change. 'There is continuity of care,' she had said, 'but there is also getting in a rut! Poor Madame Chaillet might appreciate a new face. She is still waiting for her husband to get leave from his job in order to visit her more often. It seems to be getting her down, and you, Mademoiselle Bonnet, look as if the view of the east side of the ward might do you some good!'

Surely she couldn't have noticed the tension when Jacques is around? Isabelle wondered. She bitterly regretted the night they had spent together. If she hadn't *given* herself to him like that then perhaps she wouldn't be feeling this way now—pained, thwarted, rebellious and appalled at the strength of her own feelings.

It just wasn't reasonable or rational to feel this way for someone who—as she kept telling herself quite fruitlessly—she knew so little. It was a brief, foolish thing. An infatuation. *It would go away!* It *had* to!

And, no, Simone Boucher could not have noticed. The

head nurse often seemed to be far too brisk and brittle to attain that level of sensitivity, and yet… There was more to her than met the eye, and Isabelle decided with a firmness born of desperation that she would have to be more careful about disguising her feelings. Her head, for example, must no longer swivel of its own accord when she heard Jacques's voice in the corridor.

As it had just done now, following Dr Lefevre's question. 'That was Dr Ransan going by,' Isabelle said, 'towards Room Two, which is where he has Michelle Drapeau.'

'The CF girl, waiting for a transplant?'

'Yes. She had a false alarm two weeks ago. She was admitted and ready to go when the donor family changed their minds.'

'Why is she still here, then?'

'He decided to keep her in to try and improve her lung function and general health a little so she'll be stronger if another donor comes up.'

And so she'll still be alive. Isabelle didn't say this, but both she and Dr Lefevre knew it. The latter would see cystic fibrosis patients herself in the paediatric ward as the digestive system was also heavily affected by this genetic disease.

'She's hanging on?' Maryse Lefevre asked.

'So far.'

'There's certainly a commotion.' There was Jacques charging down the corridor again and shouting staccato orders at Madame Boucher, who was snapping along in his wake. Isabelle's heart turned over again.

I *hate* him for making me feel like this!

'Could it be another potential donor?' Dr Lefevre murmured.

It was. Two weeks had passed since the earlier disappointment, but this time everything seemed to be going ahead. Consent was definite. Cross-matching had been successful, the donor organ had been flown in from Paris and Michelle herself was quickly prepped and taken to Theatre for this still-radical procedure.

Isabelle was very much on the periphery of the drama. Her own patients today were not seriously ill, needing only routine care and a little information about the procedures they would be undergoing today and tomorrow. Consequently, it was very hard not to think more of Jacques and to wonder how Michelle Drapeau's transplant was going.

The chest specialist did not perform the surgery himself, of course, but he would be closely involved in preparing for it and following up on it, as well as being present if he possibly could as the nineteen-year-old had been his patient for several years.

At least Isabelle was not alone in her curiosity. The Hôpital Saint-Jean had been performing heart-lung transplants for only a year, having brought in an internationally trained surgeon from Paris to head up the transplant team, and opportunities for this particular operation were still rare enough to create a stir. Everyone exchanged information during breaks—at the nurses' station and during report and change-over at three.

'She'll be going straight to Intensive Care from Recovery, of course.'

'I saw Nicole Arnoux at lunch and she said they weren't even out of surgery yet.'

'Looking at her this morning before we knew about the new donor, I thought, "You're not going to make it through the week, my poor one!" and now this, and she'll have years left if it all goes well.'

'Dr Ransan nearly bit my head off! I didn't know she was on standby for the surgery and I tried to give her her digestive enzyme capsules ready for breakfast.'

'Funny, you hardly ever see him angry.'

'Oh, no, *ma chère,* because it only takes *once* and then you'll do anything not to have it happen again! He knows it, too, which is why he can get further with humour and that quiet, ominous politeness of his than his wretched Remy can get with a cinematic scene of heroic proportions.'

'Sh! Here he comes!'

'Dr Chapuis?'

'No, the other one...'

Isabelle stared down, having contributed little to the discussion. Now she knew she was flushing, which was ridiculous because all that had happened was that Jacques had stridden from the lift and was coming towards them.

'I thought you'd all like to know,' he said. 'The surgery was successful and she's up in Intensive Care now. I'm on my way there. It was touch and go at one stage. Some bad bleeding at the transplant site. But it's over now, and the excellent care she's had in here during the past two weeks has made her strong enough, I'm sure, to pull through these first risky days. Thank you, everyone!'

'When will she be allowed visitors?' asked Chantal Prost, who was taking over from Isabelle in a few minutes. 'I got to know her quite well down on Paediatrics a couple of years ago and I'd like to see her.'

'Leave it for a day or two,' Jacques advised. 'I'll let you know tomorrow after she's through the first twenty-four hours.'

He made to leave again a moment later, and Isabelle's gaze was drawn upwards just a second too soon. Their eyes met and held across the heads of the other nurses, and he shifted a little—hesitated, as if about to add something. Then, frowning, he shook his head—just a tiny movement.

Everyone else probably thought he was simply wrestling with some knotty medical issue. Isabelle knew that he was thinking of her, but that shake of the head didn't suggest that he'd come up with anything very rosy. She glared at him, then shut her eyes and tossed her head as if that might shake the image and the memory of him from her mind.

I hate having to see him nearly every day!

And it seemed typical of her luck, fifteen minutes later, that they should meet in the lift, both on their way out of the building. The other nurses on her shift had already left, which she would have done, too, except that, after carrying a packet of longer shoelaces around with her for over a week, it had suddenly struck her as imperative that she should put them in right then to replace the current ones which she found too short.

She had to wonder about it. *Was I subconsciously hoping that it would take me exactly the same length of time to finish report and put in those shoelaces as it took him to see Michelle up in Intensive Care? No, surely not, because I don't want to see him!*

So when the lift doors opened to reveal him, travelling from the fourth to the ground floor in solitary state, she didn't bother with superfluities such as hello, and neither did he. The ride took less than a minute. Barely time for the silence between them to draw out into discomfort. But then he leaned with an economical movement towards the lift control panel and pressed the button which held the doors closed.

'Is this some exercise for your thumb?' she said as coldly as she possibly could.

'Yes, a kind of digital push-up. Isabelle—' Any humour in his response was overtaken by his rather fraught use of her name.

'Yes, Jacques?'

'I've been wanting to talk and this seems as good a place as any.'

'Really? It's a fairly unpleasant place, actually—boxy and too bright, and it smells of institutional food!'

'Isabelle…'

'Don't you dare sound *patient* with me, Jacques, as if this is *my* fault! I—I— *Take* your hand off that button!'

She batted wildly and ineffectually at his hand and couldn't have got him to move it except that he suddenly decided to let her and dropped his arm. The lift door opened a few seconds later.

'Thank you,' she said heavily, and lunged into the foyer.

'Isabelle, we need to—'

'No, we don't,' she said, trying not to make a scene. 'There's nothing we need to do. We already did far more than was necessary two weeks ago when I—stayed at your place. I'm not going to be able to forget that in a hurry!' She gave a bitter laugh. 'And it's given me quite enough to think about rather than having another juicy little scene between the two of us for me to chew over!'

She took advantage of the sudden influx of a group of visitors and darted through them to the main door. Jacques's far greater bulk prevented such a nimble action on his part and so she got away, which she felt very triumphant about until she looked back and found that he didn't even seem to be *trying* to follow her—which then, most perversely, made her yearn for his company even if it was only in order to rage at him.

So it didn't make any sense *at all* that when she heard his voice behind her just as she reached Claire's building she told him very quietly and almost reasonably to 'just please go away'.

'I'm not,' he said, equally reasonably, 'until you reassure me on one point.'

'Why on earth should I reassure you about anything at all?'

'Just let me come up,' he begged.

The man who owned the ground-floor bicycle shop appeared behind the large plate-glass window to study them at that moment, and since Isabelle knew that he often gossiped with Claire...

'All right,' she muttered. 'Just go quietly, that's all. Madame Claire is usually home at this time of day.'

They crept up like conspirators, and the sight of tall, loose-limbed Jacques on tiptoe might have made her laugh and turned her heart over if things had been different. No, be honest, the sight *did* turn her heart over but it definitely didn't make her laugh, and when they were both inside her apartment—it looked smaller, with him here—she backed against the door and glared at him, impatient for this just to be over, whatever it was.

Sensing this, he didn't waste any time. 'I wondered if... You're not pregnant, are you?'

'What?' Her attention caught by his odd tone, the words themselves had taken a moment to sink in.

'Expecting a baby, Isabelle,' he clarified drily. 'I will support you in any way that's necessary, if that's the case. I will take on the responsibility as fully and honourably as a man can, have no fear of that. I—'

'I'm not pregnant, Jacques. What on earth gave you the idea that I could be?'

'You said something about not being *able* to forget what happened two weeks ago. I thought you might have meant that you'd been given the legacy of a child from that night.'

He was holding himself very stiffly, as if he wanted to come over and touch her but knew he must not, and she thought that they must look like an odd pair the way she was pressed here against the door.

'Well, I didn't. I'm not,' she said. 'So that's a relief, isn't it?'

'You're sure? It's only been two weeks.'

'Well, no, I guess I won't know for sure for another ten days or so, but my cycle has always been regular and, as I told you at the time…' they were both thinking of it '…hormonally it would have been a very safe time for me.'

'Hormonally… Stranger things have happened, Isabelle.'

'Too true. Only you didn't seem to be taking that into consideration at the time,' she flashed at him hotly. 'Then you were quite happy to accept my assurance that things were safe.'

There was a silence. His eyes narrowed and then, shockingly, he laughed, a twisted sound. 'You're right! It's funny what lengths we can go to to deceive ourselves when we want to, isn't it?'

The coarse humour hurt horribly, and she was almost winded at the realisation that he could dismiss their night together in those terms. I thought I was hurt before, but I was wrong. I'd been spared the worst of it till now because I still thought that at least the night *meant* something to him.

Despite everything, I thought there was something heroic in the way he was restraining himself for his father's sake, but now… If the night itself meant that little then this isn't hard for him at all. That talk of Romeo and Juliet meant nothing. I'm not Juliet to a nobler, more adult Romeo. I'm just another stupid girl who's slept with a man and fallen in love, only to find it was nothing to him at all…

'There's no self-deception on my side,' she told him in a hard little voice. 'I'm just thanking my lucky stars that your father's feelings—since supposedly they're so important to you—have given us a way out. Now go, would you, please? And if by any slim chance I *am* pregnant I'll send you the bill for a termination!'

He went white. 'You don't mean that, Isabelle.'

'Oh, right! Easy for you to have scruples!'

'Isabelle…' It was a groan, and his face was twisted so that, despite everything, she longed to go and smooth it with her hands—to comfort the tall man as if he were a boy.

She resisted this pitiable impulse however, and said between clenched teeth, 'Get out, Jacques.'

He did, and then she was wretched enough a few moments later to clatter down the stairs after him, just so that she could watch that long body as it strode up the street and disappeared amongst the late afternoon crowds of students.

When she went back up the stairs Claire was just ushering Jeanne out of her apartment and of course she had to stop and talk, although she had no desire to see *anyone* right now, let alone these two with their extravagant concern for her welfare and their lifelong connection to Jacques.

It was just over two weeks since Jeanne had been discharged from hospital and the immediate crisis in her health had passed for the moment under the new regime of oxygen, a diuretic to reduce fluid build-up and a drug to stimulate her failing heart. She was exquisitely dressed and made-up as usual, but her movements were frail and slow and Isabelle instinctively turned to help her down the stairs, with Claire supporting Jeanne's other arm.

There was a taxi waiting outside, and as Jeanne climbed into it she kissed Isabelle warmly and said, 'Come to dinner very soon, with Claire. Friday?'

'I'd love to,' Isabelle promised, dragging a smile onto her face that didn't want to be there at all.

Alone with Claire again a minute later, things weren't so easy. After that painful scene between herself and Jacques in his office two weeks ago she had confessed to her elderly mentor, 'You were right, Madame Claire.'

'That you should have waited?'

'That he'd be angry. I doubt waiting would have helped. He—he feels very deeply about it all.'

'Yes, he always has. He's the type that is unshakably loyal to those he loves,' Claire had answered.

That viewpoint had given a certain nobility to the necessary distance between them, but now...

I won't tell her how sordid it all seems after what he just said. Thank goodness she didn't see him just now because I think I'd simply have burst into tears... No! I'd have nipped into her apartment to grab a nice, priceless piece of Sèvres pottery to chuck at him!

ISABELLE'S PERIOD CAME, as predicted, ten days later, creating an ambivalence that she found appalling in herself. Beneath it all, was there a part of her that had actually *wanted* his child? And was her sense of being tied in knots about him responsible for these cramps that were racking her? She didn't usually suffer from them.

Carine Faivre gave her a couple of tablets for the pain and she gulped them with about two sips of water as she sat at the nurses' station, filling out report...only to look up and see Jacques himself watching her from across the untidy desk.

'You have a headache?'

'No. Cramps.'

She returned to her report, wondering when he'd stop these little attempts to soften her up with small talk. Couldn't he see that she didn't want to? Couldn't he see there was no point? And why couldn't *she* get a firmer fix on the dislike she was trying so hard to feel for him? Her blunt, brief replies to him masked a deep hunger to be with him which she *would not* give in to!

Keeping her head down for the next half-hour and then spending another hour with her patients before the change of shift, she was sure he must be long gone, but as she left the main building on her way home and twisted into a side street there he was and she realised he must have deliberately waited for her.

'Cramps,' he said. 'So you really aren't pregnant...'

'I told you I wasn't,' she returned coldly. 'It's a sheer relief to me, as you can imagine, and I don't know why you keep harping on about it!'

There was a silence and then, as if goaded to breaking point, he seethed, 'Why do you act as if this is hard only for you? Don't you believe me when I tell you why we can't be together?'

'No,' she told him with harsh honesty, 'I don't think I do. I did at first...'

'Then let me *show* you! Come and see for yourself why what happened thirty-five years ago is still so alive in my father's mind. I will not have you hating me for this. It's that which makes it unbearable.'

And this was so close to what she felt herself that she turned to him in surprise, her feelings written in her face quite nakedly until the sudden heat in him told her how clearly he had read her.

'You will come, then?' he said eagerly, seizing her hands.

She shook them off. 'I will. I must be mad. I don't know what this is going to prove but, OK, I'll come.'

'Tomorrow. We will visit my father's shop. My mother will be there, too. I won't confront them with who you are.'

'All right...' The words dragged tiredly from her.

'This isn't important to you?' he demanded.

'Oh, yes!' She smiled faintly. 'It's important!'

'That's all I need to hear.'

'But I wish it wasn't!'

They looked at each other, then he grated an oath and wheeled away to cross the street. 'Tomorrow, then, Isabelle? I'll come to your apartment at four.'

'I'll be waiting.'

Waiting and, very foolishly, *hoping*…Maybe something could be salvaged out of this. The hope got out of control before she'd realised that it was happening. Perhaps because they had had such a good day on the ward.

Sister Marie-Pierre had been discharged, a day or two earlier than everyone was really happy about as her lungs had been very slow to clear. They all suspected, and had reported said suspicions to Dr Ransan, that she would return too soon to her garden and other labours, but she had been growing very restless.

When her discharge was finally approved she was patently relieved but then she apologised for this, expressed a very endearing fear that they would think she was being critical of their care and gave them all her blessing, very warm and full of her faith.

'I'm not very religious,' said flirty young Alix Dumont, 'but when someone like Sister Marie-Pierre blesses me like that it's hard not to feel…well, *blessed!*'

Yvette Chaillet was doing much better and her kidneys were holding up. Madame Guillaume's series of gastric tests had come back negative, while Madame Boillot's colonoscopy was actually *positive* for surgically removable pre-cancerous lesions, and this had pleased the shameless old hypochondriac so much that she forgot to complain about what they now knew to be real discomfort for the rest of the day. She could scarcely wait for news of when her surgery would take place.

'I'll be in a lot of pain,' she announced with an impossible blend of lugubriousness and glee. 'So I do hope those nurses in the surgical ward understand my condition the way you do here on *dear* Ward Seven, *mesdemoiselles!*'

'A compliment from her isn't quite as good as a blessing from Sister Marie-Pierre,' Alix said in an aside to Isabelle, 'but it's definitely more of a miracle!'

And the news on Michelle Drapeau that filtered down

from the heart ward was good, too, ten days after her transplant. Stable condition, still some chest-tube discomfort but little pain at the surgery site now.

'Jacques will be so pleased,' Isabelle said to Alix, without stopping to think.

'Oh, so it's Jacques, now, is it?'

'No, it isn't. I mean, it's Dr Ransan. For some reason, I—'

'Don't worry. I won't tell.'

'Just a crush,' Isabelle told her lightly, realising that further denial would only add fuel to the flames. 'It'll pass in a week.'

'Mine did,' Alix answered. 'I mean, he's great but I like men my own age when it comes to a real relationship.'

'Oh, so do I!' I wish I did because I've definitely got some chinks in my armour at the moment.

Such as thinking that perhaps a few miracles were in the air of the ward after Sister Marie-Pierre's stay, hovering like friendly bats, and that one of them would cling to her shoulder and come with her this afternoon to François Ransan's cheese shop, where Jacques would suddenly see that his father *wasn't* bound up in the past after all and would apologise abjectly for that crass, cruel comment about deceiving himself on the issue of contraception the night they'd slept together…

Several rosy scenarios followed. Needless to say, they didn't come to pass.

She was waiting for him as promised, dressed in black boot-leg pants and a cream sweater as the day was clear but chilly. He seemed tense, and she knew that she was. He'd walked here, and she was down at street level already so that she saw him striding towards her, his hands thrust into the pockets of an oatmeal-coloured jacket worn over dark pants.

We match…she thought at first, then as he got closer, No, we don't. Look at his face!

Her own eager, nervous smile drained away—hopefully before he had seen it.

'There was a phone message from my mother earlier,' he told her, 'but I haven't had a chance to return her call. Madame Trimaille said she sounded agitated.'

'I'm surprised Madame Trimaille's ears are equipped for detecting such nuances in human emotion,' Isabelle joked.

Bad idea. He'd evidently forgotten their shared theories on his receptionist's non-human molecular composition.

She saw now that he really was concerned, and prompted, 'Agitated?'

'Upset, I imagine. Sorry!' He laughed briefly. 'Agitated was Madame Trimaille's word, and perhaps you're right about her emotional sensors. If this is about what I think it is…'

'Should we leave it for another day?' she suggested. 'Meeting your parents, I mean.'

'No! Meeting them today will probably be quite repellently appropriate!'

He was striding so fast that she could barely keep up, and could only glimpse his profile at an angle. It looked forbidding, preoccupied, and all the promise she had so foolishly allowed herself to find in the day ebbed and then disappeared entirely.

He wasn't looking for a plausible excuse to see her; he wasn't planning any sort of apology; he wasn't hoping that a meeting between herself and François Ransan would break down barriers. He meant just what he had said—that doing this would convince her as thoroughly as he was convinced himself that past family history was an insurmountable obstacle. Whatever he had meant about deceiving himself on the possibility of pregnancy seemed merely a confusing incongruity now, and she didn't hate him for it any more. They'd both said wild things that they hadn't meant. Maybe it was just that.

Is it really pitiful that I'm so eager and able to forgive him? she wondered miserably.

CHAPTER SEVEN

THEY crossed the river at the Pont L'Eveque, which bridged the apex of the Loque's omega-shaped coil around the old city, then soon turned off along a street that angled away from the water like a dog's hind leg. It wasn't a particularly pretty street but was prosperous enough, containing several restaurants and small shops with apartments and one or two offices above.

Isabelle saw the sign just ahead, FRUITIÈRE—ÉPICERIE FINE. Not a fruit shop, as the name sounded to an English ear, but—here in the Jura—a shop that sold cheese. She didn't have time to see much more than the name before they were inside and surrounded by the pungently savoury smells of cheeses, sausages, pâtés and olives.

A dark woman with features so intense that one didn't notice at first their essential plainness straightened from behind the counter, saw Isabelle first and began in a polite voice that was high with strain, 'May I help—?' Then she saw her son. 'Jacques! Did you get my message?'

She came round to him and gripped his arms as he bent to receive her kiss. She was solid but small, and he towered over her.

'Yes, half an hour ago,' he said.

'You didn't phone back!'

'I tried. The line was busy. Then I couldn't wait. I was meeting Isabelle, you see.'

'Isabelle…? *Bonjour, mademoiselle!*'

'She is from Canada. A nurse at the hospital. I promised

to teach her the correct way to buy cheese.' A smoking, apologetic glance at Isabelle told her that he disliked this fiction as much as she did, but then his mother dragged his attention back again.

'He's on the phone to the lawyer again now. He's—' She broke off and looked at Isabelle. '*Mademoiselle*, excuse me if I do not help you at once. I must speak to my son. We have a new sausage that you might like to try. See, there are samples cut already here on this plate. Please… Make yourself at home.'

'What has happened, *Maman?* Is it—?'

'The will, of course,' she muttered harshly, trying but failing to keep her voice down in her emotion. 'The lawyer says there is no hope—that our contesting it would fail. The shop goes to *Madame's* wretched son, who will sell it over our heads to someone who will want to run it themselves, and your father will be out in the cold after she *promised* him she would specify that he was to be given a mortgage and first option to buy. And of course he's— Here he comes.'

A man, as tall as Jacques—*too* tall for this neat little shop—and as impressive in a darker, more tortured way, lurched from the back room into position behind the counter and slurred, 'Some cheese, *mademoiselle?*'

'Not from you, François,' Giselle Ransan came in. 'You're too dr— You couldn't hold a knife.'

Drunk, she had started to say, biting the word back just in time. She didn't need to say it, though. It was obvious, despite the deep magnetism of the man. He was handsome, with iron grey hair, a strong jaw and brown eyes that could flash as well as soften. Jacques's eyes, Isabelle realised with quite a shock, and containing the same intelligence, too. There was a chronic restlessness in that face, though, that she had never seen in Jacques's.

François Ransan ignored his wife's opinion about the

knife and produced one which did, indeed, look alarmingly
uncontrolled in his hand. 'Now, *mademoiselle*...'

'Not now, *Papa,*' Jacques said in a dark, strained voice
which Isabelle had not heard before. 'She's with me.'

'All the more reason, then, why she should receive my
f-full atten-ten—' He swore, and got the word out at last,
'Attention.'

'Look, forget the cheese! Did the lawyer say—?'

'No, Jacques,' his mother interrupted desperately, 'we
can't discuss it now. François, you must lie down...
Jacques, he was supposed to pick up a consignment of
cheeses today from Monsieur Perrin in Crozelay, and we
need them for two orders being collected first thing tomorrow.'

'I'll go. Is that what you want?' Jacques offered.

'Yes! Take our car. I must remain in the shop and he's
in no state to drive.' She turned distractedly. 'Forgive me,
mademoiselle! What will you think?'

Her strong, intriguing face worked and then settled again.
She thrust a bunch of keys into Jacques's hand.

'The old cheese-maker, Gerard Perrin?' he asked.

'Yes. You remember the way?'

'Oh, yes.'

'Get him to come and see you,' François came in fuzzily.
He was now leaning heavily against the doorway, in a careless, familiar way which suggested that he had resorted to
this position before. 'Coughs his lungs out. When he's not
making cheese he's chain-smoking. Cancer, for sure. I've
told him, but he won't listen. After all, what am I? A doctor? Not I, and never will be. If I could go back thirty-five
years and *twist* the arm of Fate...'

'Go, François, before a customer sees you like this!'
Madame Ransan begged, and Isabelle saw Jacques's jaw
tighten and his fists clench as he stared into the floor as if
his look might ignite it.

He missed something though—a brief stroking of Giselle Ransan's hand down her husband's back that contained a wealth of care and forgiveness.

They love each other far more than Jacques realises, Isabelle thought.

François Ransan had disappeared into the back room at last, and they all heard the squeak and plock of a cork being twisted from a wine bottle, and then the untidy slosh of liquid into a glass.

'Monsieur Perrin will have the order ready?' Jacques asked, his voice still strained.

'Oh, yes. He was expecting François this morning. And here is our payment in this envelope. You must have him write a receipt.'

A customer entered and Isabelle saw Madame Ransan school the worry away from her face to make way for a painfully stretched smile. 'Another time, *mademoiselle,*' she said distractedly to Isabelle, and then Jacques had swept them both out of the shop.

'You got even more than I bargained for,' he growled. 'I'll drop you home. Unless… Frankly, I could do with some company. I'm—'

'Of course I'll come, if you'd like.' It hurt her to see how much he cared about all this.

'Thanks.' He touched her arm, and she longed to return the gesture with a squeeze and then nestle against him, but he'd moved away, as if regretting the contact, and now they had reached the car—a plain white Renault, parked crookedly right up against the wall of a small alley.

'You'll have to get in through the driver's side door,' he said, and held it open for her to do so, which made her very aware of her own movements as she slipped past him and negotiated the awkward climb. They hadn't even touched, and yet her skin was singing.

After this, they said nothing for quite some time. Their

route took them back over the Pont L'Eveque to skirt the river, then they climbed out of the Loque's valley to the farmlands beyond the city—a landscape of rolling hills, stretches of forest, mainly pine, fields of grazing cattle and small stone villages, each punctuated by a reaching spire.

They had turned off the main road and onto a much smaller route before he spoke at last. 'I'm sorry about that, Isabelle.'

'Wasn't it the point of the exercise?' she suggested carefully.

He gave a short laugh. 'Yes, but…'

'I gather the shop is to be sold over his head when he was hoping to be able to buy it himself. That makes feelings run high. I thought your mother seemed like a very strong woman.'

'She is. Strong and loving and endlessly forgiving.'

'There's no way the money can be raised for the shop?'

'That's what I'm thinking about. I can't see a way. Short of selling my practice or my apartment, neither of which my parents would countenance. And my sisters are still establishing themselves in Paris. They have nothing to spare.'

'What I don't understand is…surely your grandparents were fairly well off. This mysterious sum of money— cash—that was supposedly stolen can't have been their sole asset!'

'No, you're right. It was forty thousand francs, I believe, but, no, the bulk of my grandfather's capital was lost after he died, when my rather foolish grandmother decided to play investor on the strength of her intuition. Virtually all of it had been lost by her death in 1978, and even their house had to be sold then to pay off creditors. No, there's only one person in the Ransan family who could afford this, I think, and that's Tante Jeanne.'

'Jeanne, yes!'

'But my father would never take that much from her, and especially not now. I'll have to apply to the bank myself and see if I can qualify for another mortgage, but it's doubtful. We won't talk about it any more, Isabelle.'

'All right.'

'In any case, we're here.'

He pulled into the yard of a typical Jura farmhouse, with low, heavy eaves and stacks of wood piled ready for winter around the outside walls. The place must have been quite old, but had obviously been modernised, and there was a neatly painted sign out the front reading, FROMAGERIE ARTISANALE. TASTE OUR 'CROZELIN' CHEESE!

The little shop was dimly lit and unoccupied at the moment, but they heard sounds through a back door and Jacques went to call, '*Monsieur!* Monsieur Perrin? We're here to pick up an order!'

A few minutes later an elderly man came through, muttering and clutching at his back. He peered at them, coughed and said, 'Order?'

'Yes, I'm Jacques Ransan. It's a while since we've met, *monsieur,* but I've come for my parents' consignment of cheese.'

'Of course,' he nodded gruffly. 'Only you're late, and I nearly forgot. I've been cleaning. Come through and help me load the boxes. It's all packed.'

They followed him and Isabelle was fascinated by the sight of the huge metal milk vats and old-fashioned cheese presses, the former clean and shining and empty. Cheeses, too. She knew enough about French cheese by this time to recognise the big flat wheels of Comte and smaller wheels of Morbier, with its distinctive layer of grey ash through the centre, but couldn't guess at the other shapes and colours—small bricks and cylinders, little balls, huge logs of waxy-skinned cheeses like wooden beams.

There was even a milking stool, part of an exhibit of

antique dairy equipment in one corner. She smiled at it, thinking of those silly moments with Jacques, then caught his eye and found that he was smiling too—that quick, open spread of his firm lips, revealing white teeth, that she'd been drawn to right from the start. But the smile drained away as quickly as it had come. He schooled his face and she remembered that it was an impossible situation.

'You're not making any cheese today?' she asked Monsieur Perrin, as a distraction.

'My milk is delivered very early in the morning and I make it then. That way, when people come to taste and buy later in the day, I can give a little tour with no fears about contaminating the milk. Would you like to taste some of my cheeses, *mademoiselle,* and to hear how they are made?'

He looked so eager that Isabelle couldn't say no, and she was rather amused when he left Jacques to haul the four heavy wooden boxes packed closely with cheeses and began to hover over her, feeding her like a baby with slivers of several different tastes as he described how each one was produced.

Several times he had to break off in order to cough behind a clean white handkerchief, having turned carefully away from the cheese counter before clearing his throat with a great deal of effort, and Isabelle remembered François's rambling opinion on the old man's health. That chest certainly didn't seem good, nor did that gesture he made frequently—irritably rubbing at his ribs with a tight fist, as if trying to massage away pain.

'Please excuse me, *mademoiselle…*' was all he said about it. 'Now, the one you are eating at the moment is made with the addition of chicory—an experiment of sorts. Monsieur Ransan!' he said, turning to Jacques, who had finished loading the car now. He had evidently forgotten, or perhaps had never known, that François Ransan's son was a doctor. 'You must taste it, too.'

Jacques did so, and Isabelle watched the slow, appreciative movement of his mouth. He was so very French! She could see that Monsieur Perrin was pleased at his sober concentration.

It's like tasting wine, she realised. Perhaps I asked too many questions and didn't say enough about the cheese itself.

'Have you written down your methods, Monsieur Perrin?' Jacques wanted to know.

'No need. I keep them in my head.' He tapped this organ proudly. 'I'm not much for writing, but I don't forget my methods.'

'But for others. It would be tragic if this craftsmanship was lost, *monsieur*. And you know you can't last for ever.'

'Oh, but no one's interested in these old ways. They all want the pasteurised milk and every cheese to taste the same nowadays.'

'Do you know, I think you're wrong!' Jacques argued energetically. 'There's been a surge of interest in the past few years.'

'True, there is a young chap over in Epenouse, selling his own cheese made this way. "Spinosien", he calls it, and "P'tit Gilles". He doesn't do a bad job,' Monsieur Perrin conceded. 'Perhaps I should write it all down but, as I say, I'm not much good with a pen.'

'But you can talk, can't you?'

'When this cough's not troubling me!'

'How about into a tape? Would you be willing to have it recorded?'

'What, me? My old rasping voice, gabbling on about cheese?' He laughed comfortably.

'I'm serious, *monsieur*. There is a programme at the moment at the hospital to record the important memories of some of our local people. Things are changing, you know…'

'Oh, don't I know!' He laughed and coughed again.

'I'd really like you to come in and take part. One of my colleagues—'

'But with this cough of mine…'

'We'll look at that, too. My father says you've been neglecting it, and you may remember that I'm a doctor…a chest specialist.'

'Eh?' He blinked, and then uttered a long, 'Oh! *Non! Les médecins!* It's always the same! I'd forgotten you were a doctor, and now you're tricking me into coming to see you so you can tell me I smoke too much—which I know already!'

'Monsieur Perrin…'

'*Non et non!* I thank you for your interest in my cheese-making, *Monsieur le Docteur,* but my lungs are my own business and you won't get your hands on me, poking and testing.'

'Well, you may change your mind,' Jacques responded carefully, 'and, if you do, here is my card. Phone me, too, if you'd like to make a tape. We can do that even if you don't want a chest exam.'

'You're too sly! I don't trust you! I think we'll leave the taping business alone, if you don't mind!'

Jacques only nodded. The atmosphere was uncomfortable now, and the rest of their transaction was completed in a quick and rather formal way. Monsieur Perrin was still muttering about '*les médecins*' when they left.

In the car, Jacques said bluntly and decisively, 'I mismanaged that.'

'No, you didn't,' Isabelle told him, quite as firmly. 'Your father had already told you he was refusing to see anyone.'

'But I didn't persuade him differently.'

'Because he's as stubborn as a mule,' she pointed out.

'The fact that he still makes his cheeses the traditional way, marvellous though that is, shows that he's resistant to change and new ideas, don't you think?'

'So it's actually very arrogant of me to think that I could just walk in and change a lifelong attitude to his health?'

'*Very* arrogant! The way it's arrogant of you to think you'll stop your lazier students from sleeping in lectures when they've done it from time immemorial.'

'You agree with Monsieur Perrin's views on the medical profession, then?'

'Absolutely! All nurses do. Arrogant pigs, the lot of you!'

'Ah, and you don't think that's perhaps a necessary quality when there's so much at stake with every professional decision we make?' he countered energetically.

She relented and grinned. 'Actually, I do. I like a little arrogance in a...doctor.'

She had almost said 'man'. He knew it, too. In fact, they were quite definitely flirting, which wasn't part of the programme. Dangerous! She should be sitting here behind a carefully constructed wall of distance. The purpose of the afternoon had been accomplished an hour ago at the shop. She'd seen what he'd wanted her to see.

She could see that Cousin François and Jacques were father and son—both magnetic, oaken men, but in one there was something flawed while the other looked as if he could withstand life's blows much better. François Ransan was not strong enough to forgive a liaison between his son and his enemy's daughter. Jacques Ransan *was* strong enough to put aside the possibility of love for his father's sake.

But meeting these long-lost cousins, François and Giselle, had only brought her closer to Jacques—had taken away her anger at him without her even being aware that it had happened, and had woven the strands of her own life far more tightly into the fabric of his, she realised now.

There was a sense of belonging to Vesanceau and to the Ransans that was very bitter, the way things stood.

I should ask him to take me home because he's told me there's no future in this, and I can see it now for myself, but every time I'm with him I rebel against it…

But she *didn't* ask, and a few minutes later he said restlessly, 'Mind if we drive a bit and don't go straight back?'

'You've remembered another errand?'

'No. I just need more air…more space.'

'Then, no, I don't mind. Space…sounds good.'

He'd spoken the word with such a hunger that he'd given her the same appetite, and she leaned her head back on the rather hard padded shoulder of the seat and gave herself up to speed and motion and the landscape flashing by.

They regained the main road to Vesanceau but stayed on it for only a few minutes, before taking another side road which followed the valley of the River Meleze and soon began to climb. It was an exhilarating and stunningly lovely route, with the mid-October foliage just beginning to turn and the river glimpsed below in patches of jade and dark blue-green in the late light.

Isabelle wound down the stiff window handle to let in a blast of air, and Jacques asked lightly, 'Blowing the cobwebs out?'

'Blowing everything out. It's good!'

'It is. There's a look-out just ahead. Would you like to stop?'

'Yes, please!'

They came to it a few minutes later and he veered the small car into the even smaller space just off the road, edged by a low stone wall. She climbed out and almost ran to the parapet, eager to stretch her legs, feel the freshness and discover the architecture of that village piled above the bend in the river below.

The drop from where she stood was sharp, almost cliff-like, through steep forest straight to the river—a distance of hundreds of feet—but the yawning void was exhilarating rather than frightening.

'It's fabulous! So beautiful! Those houses look as if they've just grown up out of the bedrock.'

'I used to cycle up here in my teens,' Jacques answered, 'on a terrible old Peugeot bike. For the air.'

'Which you must have needed in vast quantities after such a climb!'

'But then the trip down…!'

'Oh, I can imagine! I have a mountain bike at home. British Columbia is a great place for cycling. In Vancouver there's a bike-way that runs along the sea-wall around Stanley Park, right on the water, past the aquarium and under Lions Gate Bridge.'

'We should do this ride together, then. It's long, you can see that. It'd take all day, but—'

'No… No, Jacques,' she came in, not sounding nearly as firm as she wanted to. 'It'd be…silly, don't you think?'

He looked at her, frowning darkly. 'Silly?' he rasped. 'What an insipid word! Yes, it would be silly. Very! And right at this moment, you know, Isabelle, I simply don't care!'

She was in his arms before she knew it, and his kiss was reckless and hotly demanding. It felt so good! Like the explosion of sweet juice in her mouth when she bit on a handful of grapes, or like flinging herself down onto a bed of soft pine needles for a lunch break during one of those arduous mountain biking trips with her friends on a Canadian spring day.

Coming home. Coming to rest. But that was only a small part of it. It was like taking flight, too, as if they'd both grown wings and soared off this rough stone wall where she was leaning the backs of her knees to swoop and dive through the valley above the tumbling and looping water.

The breeze was fresh and cool but here, in each other's arms, it was *warm*.

As his mouth plundered hers more and more deeply she heard his need vibrating in his throat, amid groans and cries that she echoed fully. His hands explored her shape urgently—searing down her back, cupping her buttocks and her breasts, kneading handfuls of her lush hair. She buried her face in his neck and felt the mad racing of his pulse, then returned to his mouth until her lips were swollen. Her eyes opened, seizing on blurred images of his profile—his dark lashes, his high temples—before closing again to block out the distraction of sight so that only sensation was left.

Insistently, though, the voice of sanity began to clamour within her mind. And sanity brought anger. *He* had told her that this was impossible after that one wonderful night they had shared together. *He* had convinced her of the deep, genuine nature of the chasm between them, and now he was casually tossing that conviction aside. For how long? A few moments, she knew. Just as long as it took for this unbrookable madness to be made manageable.

Funny, though. Anger was certainly no barrier to passion. She returned each ravaging movement of his mouth, taste for taste, while her throat grew tighter and tighter and her hands more claw-like as they raked his back and buttocks until she knew she must be leaving long, inflamed marks.

Tears came. Tears of anger that she blinked back and blinked back until she gave up the attempt and just let them course down, starting to sting her cheeks as they ran towards the place where her mouth was joined to his so that she began to taste salt.

He must have tasted it, too. 'What is it, Isabelle?'

'You know damn well what it is! You told me...you *convinced* me...that this couldn't happen. Do you know how hard that was for me after I'd spent the night with you?'

'No harder than it was for me—'

'Yeah, right!' she crowed sarcastically, not believing him for a moment. 'And now you're *doing* this, making me feel it all—! I don't *want* it. You've said it's over. All right! It's over! You've had me in bed, which was your goal at the time. Be satisfied with that! Believe me, in my rational moments I couldn't be happier about it. *I* don't want any more from you!'

Pent up, she splayed her fingers and pushed hard on his chest, throwing herself away from him at the same time. Since Jacques was strong enough to remain anchored where he stood, she was the one to move—backwards. Only she'd forgotten that they stood at the edge of a dramatic drop, with only a wall that came just above her knees for protection.

Arching back against the empty air and glimpsing one stark image of a crooked, gaping sky merging into the yawning valley, she screamed, closed her eyes and then felt the desperate, clawing reach of his long arms.

CHAPTER EIGHT

'ISABELLE...*Nom de Dieu!* Isabelle!'

Shaking, she felt the hammer of his heart against her ear as he held her tightly against his chest.

'It's all right. I'm all right,' she told him dizzily, gripping him with stiffened hands.

Obviously she was. In retrospect, it hadn't even been a particularly close thing. Even had she fallen, she would have sprawled painfully on the wall, grazing and jarring her back, but the rough stone would have broken her trajectory so that Jacques would have had plenty of time to drag her to safety. As it was, his arms had reached her much sooner and there was just a scrape of grit and moss against the backs of her pant legs. Now, though, they were clinging to each other like passengers on a Titanic life-boat, which was incongruous, given the tirade she had just unleashed on him.

'I'm sorry,' he was saying through a tight mouth.

'It wasn't your fault.'

'It was! I had no right to touch you. It's over, as you say.' He had released her now, and his narrowed gaze was flicking over her. There was something unreadable and frightening in the depths of his brown eyes. Anger? 'I should not have brought you up here at all,' he said decisively, 'Nor to see Monsieur Perrin. We'll go back straight away.'

'OK.' Her breathing was still coming in high, shallow

pants, while his chest rose and fell with more control but equal strength of feeling.

He opened the passenger door for her and it creaked, punctuating their silence. Another car went by, heading down, and something about their tight body language must have caught the driver's attention because he slowed and called from his open window, '*Ça va?*'

'*Oui, oui, ça va,*' Jacques answered. He manufactured a reassuring smile with amazing speed and waved the man on.

Half an hour later they were pulling up once again outside his parents' shop. They'd barely spoken during the drive. Isabelle supposed bleakly that there simply wasn't anything more to say. Jacques was lost in thought, though, and she couldn't help feeling horribly shut out, when just a few weeks ago they'd read each other so well. Or was that just an illusion born of raging desire?

'I'll help you bring in the cheeses,' she told him woodenly.

'No, I'll get my father.'

But François Ransan had evidently put the past couple of hours to good use, and could barely stand, although he insisted on coming out and then snatched the car keys angrily from his son's hand.

Jacques's mother followed in his wake. 'I'll do it, François. There are only four boxes. Between Jacques and me, we can—'

'Out of my way. *I* am still capable of lifting a box, I think!'

But his wavering hand couldn't get the key into the lock of the car boot at first and he swore. Then at last the boot lid flew open. The boxes of cheese, though, proved too much, and grimly Jacques came beside him to stack all four one on top of the other and bring them inside.

They were heavy, extremely so, and Isabelle could see

the cords in his neck standing out and the muscles in his forearms, revealed by rolled sleeves, bulging. Her heart lurched. He should have divided the load into two trips, at least. He was crazy to push his limits like that! The stack of boxes teetered higher than his head. The splintery sides must have dug painfully into his hands, too, but he gave no sign of it and didn't even glance at his father, who was glowering after him.

'You see! You *see?* Look what your son does for you!' said Giselle Ransan wildly to her husband, then turned on her heel to seek refuge in the shop.

The big man shrugged, then lurched to the driver's side door of the car and managed to fold himself sufficiently to get inside. Isabelle was too intent at first on trying to make herself invisible to realise what he intended, sensing as she did how much it pained Jacques's mother to have her husband's behaviour witnessed by a stranger like this.

Then she registered what he was doing and thought starkly, Drive? In his condition? He can't!

She took a step forward. 'No—!' But she was powerless.

The engine gunned just as Jacques appeared in the shop door again, and with three uncontrolled and violent manoeuvres of the vehicle, François had attained the street. He began to accelerate, misjudged the movement with his foot on the pedal and, within seconds, had rammed into an iron lamppost, crushing the front of the vehicle as if it were made of aluminum foil.

'*Thank God!*' came Jacques's voice, dark, deliberate and intense.

'*What?*' She turned to him in disbelief.

Jacques explained abruptly, 'He would have killed someone if he'd got much further. But he wasn't going fast enough just then to have killed himself.'

'Oh, Jacques…' You make it so hard for me to be angry with you…

Despite what Jacques had said, the big man wasn't moving at the wheel, and Giselle Ransan had appeared again, shrieking as she saw the crushed front of the car. 'François! François!'

Jacques was beside him now. '*Papa! Papa!* Speak to me!'

'Wha—? What happened? Aie! My jaw!'

'You tried to drive. You hit the lamppost.'

Isabelle and Giselle were both beside the driver's door as well, and Giselle shrieked again as she saw blood coming from her husband's mouth.

'Let's get him inside,' Jacques said. 'I don't think it's serious. Did he lose consciousness?'

'I don't know. He didn't move for a few moments, but perhaps that was just disorientation and shock.'

'We'll check for any evidence of head injury. Meanwhile, he definitely has a broken jaw. Maybe some teeth gone. What's in your mouth, *Papa?* Anything besides blood?'

'What? No…' He produced a handkerchief, but when he tried to press it to his face again he gave a groan of pain.

'Isabelle, there's a first-aid box in the back of the shop. My mother will show you. Get out some swabs. His nose is bleeding now as well, and beginning to swell. Broken, too, I suspect.'

'Concussion?' his mother asked. 'Head injuries? Oh, *mon Dieu!*'

'Shh, *Maman,*' Jacques soothed. 'Head injuries are very unlikely. I'm just being on the safe side. He wasn't going fast enough. It looks worse than it is. Now, please, take Isabelle to get the swabs, then let her look after you. Your legs are shaking. And phone the ambulance, will you?'

'Ambulance?'

'He's been drinking, *Maman,* I'm not taking any chances. That jaw will need to be plated, but they may want to wait until the alcohol has left his system before topping up the effect with anaesthesia. *Papa*, what's your name?' he demanded of his father.

'My name?' François grumbled. 'You know my name, you fool…'

'*I* know it,' Jacques explained patiently, 'but do *you*…? And I must check your pupils. *Papa*, humour me on this!'

'All right, I'm François Ransan and my jaw is killing me.'

'And what day is it today?'

'*Oh! Non!*' the injured man groaned.

Madame Ransan was sniffing and struggling against tears as she took Isabelle inside. 'Forgive us, *mademoiselle!* This happens rarely, but when it does… He has had disappointments in his life, you see, and I've never managed to convince him that they don't matter but, you know, he's worthy and I love him with every cell in my body… Why am I saying this to a stranger?'

'Because you're upset. Understandably! And he is too, of course, with this business of the shop,' Isabelle soothed, feeling once again that with every moment that passed she felt her link to these cousins of hers growing knottier and deeper. 'Do sit down, as Jacques said, and I'll handle everything.'

She coaxed Giselle to the couch, where a half-empty bottle betrayed the fact that François had been lying here earlier. Giselle Ransan subsided into it, still tearful and shaken, and Isabelle let go of those rounded shoulders reluctantly.

I'm starting to feel for her already. She's Jacques's mother…

'If only that wretched woman—I hate to speak ill of the dead, but she was wretched when she was alive, too—had made her will as she'd promised,' Giselle Ransan said. 'She must have kept putting it off.'

'It happens,' Isabelle answered. 'People think they're immortal.'

'No, not in this case. So needlessly cruel to keep us here hanging on that hope. "I can't last much longer," she would say, "but don't worry. All these years you have managed the place for me won't go in vain." Twenty years ago, she said it! She told us her heart wouldn't last more than a few years, but now her doctor tells us it was neglected diabetes that killed her and she didn't have a heart problem at all!'

'Please don't upset yourself by talking about it all now,' Isabelle begged, sensing a pride in Giselle Ransan that would have her bitterly regretting this frank speech tomorrow.

And all the more if she knew who I am yet I can't just leave her, and Jacques is dealing with Cousin François...

'The generations can exercise such terrible cruelty over one another,' Giselle was saying now. 'Perhaps it was her son's fault, too. Perhaps he didn't want the nuisance of holding our mortgage...'

Isabelle stopped trying to stem the flow of words, as they clearly served a healing purpose today. She brought Giselle some water, then put on a kettle to make some lemon tea. The first-aid kit was easy to find and she got out the simple supplies that would be needed until the ambulance came— swabs of cotton, tweezers, gauze and antiseptic. Next she phoned for the ambulance and was told, 'Twenty minutes.'

By this time, Jacques had brought his father inside. Shock and pain were taking hold now to make him scarcely able to walk, and Jacques's strength—both physical and emotional—was confirmed once again in the way he supported his father during the latter's slow progress and spoke steadily to him.

'Let's sit you down here on the chair. We'll close the shop, *Maman*. It's almost time anyway. No evidence of head injury, by the way. He's quite oriented in time, place and person. *Papa,* I know it hurts but I want to make sure you haven't lost a tooth without realising it, and I want to feel that jaw. Isabelle, do you have what we need? Ah, good.'

With careful tenderness he opened the distorted jaw and used the tweezers to pack swabs between teeth and cheeks, where there was swelling and bleeding.

'No missing teeth,' he announced, 'but you've cut your tongue very badly. That's where most of this bleeding is coming from.' He used swabs to check the bleeding in his father's nose, and probed gently with his fingers across its bridge to confirm, 'Broken. You've been lucky, *Papa.*'

'Lucky?' he managed.

'You're alive, and you're conscious. And you have no one else's death on your conscience,' he added starkly.

'What?'

'Think of little Thierry, four doors down. If he'd been playing on the pavement and you'd got that far before you crashed...'

'Don't, Jacques!' Giselle came in.

'You don't think he needs to hear it?'

'Not now.'

'Very well.'

'He's right, Giselle,' François growled, lifting his head and seeming suddenly much stronger and more impressive. 'Thank you, both of you, Giselle and Jacques. This was a bad day. It...it won't happen again.' Simple words but they had the sense of a vow, and Isabelle found that she believed them.

After this there was no more drama. Jacques phoned a towing company to come and take the car away. Giselle drank her tea and persuaded Isabelle to have some too. The ambulance came, and François and Giselle went off in it.

Jacques locked the shop, watched the process of hooking

up the car to the tow-truck and then walked Isabelle home. They didn't touch, of course, and their conversation was very brief and to the point.

'I'll go on to the hospital,' he said. 'My parents need me…and you don't. In fact, I imagine that, as I do, you wish you'd never laid eyes on me!'

'No, Jacques,' she told him cuttingly, 'I think our problems started *way* before that!'

IT DIDN'T GET EASIER. Their paths crossed almost daily. They had to speak to each other with sufficient command of what churned beneath to avoid mistakes over patients, and that took effort. She was angry with him, and realised that he was angry with her, which only angered her still more because what right did *he* have to feel misused?

She was assigned to Yvette Chaillet again after two weeks of dealing with gastric patients. Madame Chaillet had asked to have her back, which was nice, and Isabelle was growing quite fond of the elderly woman whose body was taking such a battering, both from her disease and from the drug that was fighting it.

Her husband, Jean, had at last been granted leave from his work and was spending several hours each day at her bedside. They seemed like a close and loving couple, and Jean was a great entertainer. He read aloud to his wife, told jokes, brought in photo albums to reminisce over and relayed scandalous stories of local crime and politics gleaned from various 'contacts' amongst the police and the mayor's staff, which had Madame Chaillet round-eyed and eager for more.

And that was a good thing because after just over four weeks on the toxic antifungal drug that would rid her body of the histoplasmosis fungus, Yvette Chaillet's kidneys had begun to fail. That meant another specialist to add to the roster of names on her chart, much mulling over numbers and the adjustment of her other medications—as well as fluid, potassium and salt restriction, and other special dietary compensations.

'The good news is that the symptoms of her disease are ebbing,' Jacques said in his best bland doctor voice to Isabelle at the nurses' station after an early morning visit on Wednesday. 'Meanwhile, I see Dr Roland wants more blood drawn.'

'I'll do it when Monsieur Chaillet gets here,' Isabelle answered in her best bland nurse voice. 'His arrival always brightens her up so wonderfully.'

'Yes, although that story he was telling her yesterday about the Chief of Police's son and the mayor's sister...'

'I know!'

'Surely it can't have been—?'

'Actually on the *steps* of the *mairie*,' Isabelle agreed.

'In his office, I could believe.'

'Or even in the foyer, if it was late enough in the day, but...'

'Definitely not the steps!' they finished together.

And laughed. Their anger had evaporated for the moment and this somehow made it impossible for her not to ask, 'How is your father?'

'Good,' he answered. 'Not too happy about his jaw, but—' He hesitated, then added in a low voice, 'I've been wanting to tell you—it gave them both a scare and seems to have made them reshuffle their priorities a bit. I'm seeing so much more love between them than I'd believed was there. The way he talked to her after his jaw was set the other night... To be honest, I'd always felt he must have married her on the rebound from—' He stopped suddenly.

'My mother,' she finished for him.

Their eyes met and darted quickly away.

'But it seems that wasn't so. It just took your mother's departure with Cousin Raoul to make him see that my

mother was there, waiting. And I find…' He leaned over
the desk towards her so that she could smell the nutty scent
of his aftershave, then he took off his glasses as they began
to slip, revealing the warm, naked depth of his eyes.

He spoke very quietly and very soberly. 'I find it does a
lot for me to discover that I'm not the product of a mis-
matched and miserable marriage after all. It's like reaching
my hands out to a pile of grey ash in the fireplace, thinking
it was dead and finding that underneath there are hot, living
coals.'

The image was very vivid. She could see those large,
lean hands of his, stretching in front of him, and immediately thought of how they had felt on her body in the passionate heat of his bed. Talk about living coals…! The heat
of her memory burned on, refusing to be extinguished by
time, reason or anger.

'Why are you telling me this, Jacques?' she murmured
pleadingly.

There was no one at the nurses' station for the moment
so they couldn't be overheard. Suddenly, she wished there
was a crowd of busy nurses here.

He stiffened and pressed the heel of one hand hard
against his forehead. 'Because I have to, Isabelle.' His long
fingers scraped roughly down the side of his face. 'Because,
of all the people in my life, *you* are the one I want to tell.
I— That's impossible, isn't it?' His teeth were clenched
now. 'Wrong!'

He wheeled around and left the nurses' station, shoving
his glasses roughly back onto his face and striding from
the ward with abrupt, angular speed, and her heart ached
for both of them.

There was a change after this day. Try as she might, she
couldn't get her anger back. And she *did* try, because she
needed that anger! Far easier to feel that than to feel what
she felt helplessly now. The walks she began to take around

the city on the weekends or in the crisp autumn evenings, for example. They always took her past his place, and she was fooling herself if she really believed that was because the bakery on the corner just beyond the archway that led to his apartment was the best in Vesanceau.

She couldn't even see his apartment through that arch, but there *was* a place she could see it from—on another street, glimpsed through a gap in the buildings—and she passed that way far too often, too.

She knew his lecture schedule at the university and the hours he kept at his professional rooms. She looked him up in the telephone directory and even once accepted coffee from one of the students she was beginning to know by sight, purely in the hope that he'd be studying medicine and she could steer the conversation towards the subject of lung diseases. Unfortunately the student's field was law, and he was distinctly and lengthily boring on the subject, which served her right!

At hospital meals she instinctively stationed herself where she could see the exclusive tables used by the doctors, and when she arrived at and departed from the hospital each day her eyes automatically flicked to the places where visiting specialists could park their cars.

She visited Michelle Drapeau, too, in the heart ward, but there she didn't have to chide herself as she deliberately picked a Thursday afternoon when she knew he would have a lecture. Michelle, although progressing as well as they'd all hoped, was still too ill to say more than a few words, none of which happened to concern her chest specialist.

The result of all this was precisely nothing, of course.

Or rather, one glimpse of him getting into his car, one sighting of him drawing the curtains in his apartment, and one very awkward session of trying *not* to watch him having lunch with Remy Chapuis, Christian Froissart, and Dr Bouladon the endocrinologist.

Then there was a particular mass on a particular Sunday morning at the Église Saint-Paul. Isabelle had taken Madame Claire, who liked to go but liked company as well. Jacques had brought his mother, who usually went to a smaller church on the other side of the river but appreciated the particular grandeur and beauty of this older place at times of special stress. François Ransan rarely came, apparently, but Jacques's sister, Thérèse, was visiting from Paris for the weekend, it seemed, with a serious boyfriend in tow, so they were there, too.

Claire pointed out the group just before the service began, as if Isabelle had needed to be told! She'd seen that tall figure coming down the centre aisle and had carefully avoided looking in that direction ever since. Wasn't that the light-coloured suit he'd worn on the occasion of their very first meeting? Why did it emphasise his height so?

Instead, she stared ahead and saw a bevy of nuns from the Monastère Saint-Claire, including Sister Marie-Pierre, grouped together at the front.

Sister Marie-Pierre was coughing again. Isabelle noticed it as soon as the congregation settled down. The old nun tried to suppress it but the dry, convulsive sound echoed in the resonant acoustics of the magnificent old church, and the whole congregation must have heard it.

After a nerve-racking time of it, Sister Marie-Pierre separated herself out from her sisters and came down the side aisle. Was she leaving? Isabelle turned to look, and saw that Jacques was making the same covert investigation, prayer-book in one hand and glasses in the other. The priest was moving to the lectern to begin his sermon, and all was quiet.

No, she hadn't left. She was standing at the back, a small, bent figure, holding a white handkerchief to her mouth and poised ready to duck out the next time a fit of coughing came on.

She should be in bed, Isabelle thought. It sounds like she's had a relapse. Should I go to her now?

Not wanting to create further disturbance, she stayed where she was but kept an occasional eye out to see that the old nun was still there at the back. Again, she saw Jacques doing the same thing.

After the service Claire would listen to no protests and swept her across the aisle to the Ransan family.

'Of course we must say hello to dear Thérèse! I haven't seen her for so long! And Giselle, and Thérèse's new young man. And Jacques, too, naturally.'

So, as the congregation milled out of the church, introductions were made, with Isabelle being presented as, 'My young friend who is renting my upstairs apartment and, of course, attending to Jacques's patients,' and just the uneasy meeting of glances between Jacques and Isabelle—and a tiny dart of acknowledgement from Claire—occurred to betray the fact that there was considerably more complexity and depth to the relationship than this.

As Isabelle had expected, Jacques's mother was ill at ease, due to the emotional circumstances of their previous meeting, and was made more so when Claire squeezed her hand and whispered, not softly enough, 'I heard about your old ogress's will. Could you not apply to Jeanne for help?'

'Ah, Madame Claire, François is too proud!' Giselle whispered back.

'Then he should not be!'

'I know. Perhaps if I went behind his back… But, in any case, with Jeanne's health failing… Let's not talk of it now when Roger is with us.'

'No, indeed. How nice to meet you, Roger! You are studying French literature, too?'

'Yes, I expect to receive my doctorate within a year or two.'

There was a little more conversation, interrupted by

greetings from other friends of Claire's who had also been at mass, then the small, redoubtable woman steered Isabelle firmly ahead—through the huge old doors and into the autumn air.

The latter had exchanged precisely nine words with Jacques, a dialogue which could have come verbatim from the first lesson of a course in conversational French, and when their hips had pressed together briefly on the way down the aisle she knew that it was only because people behind them were impatient to leave and were pushing a little. He'd wanted that contact as little as she had.

Claire was murmuring, 'What a pity about Roger!' which brought a questioning look from Isabelle. She had thought he seemed nice! Answering it, Claire explained, 'What use is a doctorate in literature to the family? Had he been a banker or a stockholder in computer software, I might have slept better at night!'

'You really lose sleep over the Ransans?' Isabelle teased idly. She was scanning the church entrance for Sister Marie-Pierre, wanting to check on her after all that coughing, but there seemed to be no sign of her...

'Lose sleep? Of course I do!' Claire was saying emotionally. 'They've been my family for fifty years! The closest thing I had, anyway, since I was an only child and lost my parents in my teens. And I regret that all I *can* do is lose sleep! I have enough money to cater comfortably for my own needs, it's true—thanks to my Felix—but no more. So as to practical help... All I've ever been able to do was give advice, you see, and that, at times, I now doubt was...'

She trailed off, dabbing at her eyes, and Isabelle felt terrible at the way her casual teasing had upset Madame Claire. But now she'd seen Sister Marie-Pierre. She squeezed Claire's arm and quickly explained her need to speak to the old nun.

'Go on, my dear,' Claire said. 'My woes will keep. I'm a silly old thing!'

'No, you're *not*, actually, but Sister Marie-Pierre is! I bet she stopped taking her antibiotics too soon! And, look, she's sitting down now with Sister Cecile, all feeble and hunched over as if she can't manage the walk back.'

Isabelle hurried across the open space in front of the church in the direction of the Roman ruins and only now caught sight of Jacques, also making his way in that direction. They met up some yards short of the pair of nuns and he said to her, 'You heard her too?'

'The whole congregation did!'

'I can guess what happened...' He reached the stone bench just ahead of Isabelle. 'You were feeling better, Sister Marie-Pierre, and so you forgot to take the rest of your pills?'

'It seemed a waste. I saved them in case someone else in the convent...'

'*Ah, non! Ma soeur!* This time I am *not* going to let you out of my hospital until your course of treatment is completely finished! Those pills were meant for you and nobody else! They are not sweets, Sister!'

'Oh, please, I don't have to go back, do I?' But then she began coughing terribly, pressed her hand to her head and muttered, 'It aches so sharply!' There were no further protests about going, only about the means of getting there.

Sister Marie-Pierre would *not* use an ambulance, 'in case there's some poor soul whose need is greater than mine.' Finally Monsignor Raphael, fresh from conducting his mass, was co-opted into transporting her there in his tiny Deux-Chevaux. First, however, he needed to change out of his vestments.

Sister Cecile had been dispatched to the Monastère to get Sister Marie-Pierre's things, and Claire had forgathered again with the Ransan group on the church steps while they all waited for Jacques and Isabelle.

'I'll go with her and Monsignor Raphael,' Jacques said. 'I was planning to make a round before lunch in any case. Roger has his car and will drive my mother and my sister home.'

So that was that…almost.

Going back to them, Isabelle found that Giselle Ransan had invited both of them to lunch which evolved into an exquisite form of torture as they all waited, at the modest but pleasant Ransan house a kilometre beyond the old city's centre, for Jacques to put in an appearance.

He never did, phoning after half an hour to say, 'Don't wait to eat. I've been detained at the hospital by another patient, but shouldn't be too long,' and then again an hour into the sumptuous Sunday feast to apologise, 'I won't make it at all. Something else has come up.'

On the way home, both drowsily replete at nearly three, Claire said to Isabelle, 'There! That worked out well, didn't it? Much more awkward if Jacques had been there.'

'Oh, yes…!' *But I wanted him there anyway.*

'This way… Giselle seems to like you very much, and even grumpy François…' Who had been marvellous today, intelligent and interesting and full of praise for his wife's cooking.

'He approves of Roger,' was Claire's explanation for this. 'That's nice for Thérèse. Now, perhaps, in time…if they become truly fond of *you*…'

'Don't, Madame Claire!' Isabelle begged. 'No plotting, please! I—I wouldn't even want it any more…'

'Hmm! Seeing them all at mass today was good. It reminded me that it's high time I had them over to a meal. You will be there, of course, and—'

'No! I won't! It can't do any good, Claire, and you have to accept that.' *If only I could accept it myself…*

CHAPTER NINE

AUTUMN had arrived in full glory, and as the leaves changed colour and fell, Isabelle set about proving to herself and to Claire—and perhaps to the man himself—that there was life after Jacques.

In desperate circumstances, one didn't spend too much time considering methods, and she chose the means to hand—male students.

After being firmly *un*flirtatious with them for some weeks, her sudden friendliness, her vibrant dark-eyed, glossy-haired looks and her exotic Canadian aura brought them flocking like flies to honey. She accepted coffee on her way home from work, and allowed herself to be mildly chatted up in the bookshop or complimented when she went to buy jeans.

She even took a ride home on the back of a motor bike so feeble and shrill that her eldest Harley-Davidson-riding brother would have teased her about it for six months afterwards. When its owner, a very well-mannered major in political studies, deposited her right at Claire's feet just as the latter was coming home from the bakery, she told him breezily that she would see him tomorrow—even though he'd already said he had a lecture that went until six.

Claire was aghast.

'But I must have a social life, Madame Claire,' Isabelle pointed out innocently. 'People my own age,' she added firmly, although this particular chap couldn't have been more than twenty, to her twenty-six. 'Guy and I have more in common than I'd have with, say, someone over thirty who was already established in his career.' Which, surely, would dampen Claire's appetite for a mission that Isabelle found too painful and too hopeless to pursue.

There did seem to be an aura of defeat about Claire as Guy sputtered off, with a clumsy change of gear. Just in case, though, Isabelle made a point of continuing energetically with her new social life and soon had invitations from female students, as well as males, for casual evenings at a restaurant or in someone's crowded apartment.

It was fun…great fun…and some of the older students, such as Nadine and Anny, started to become real friends, yet she always went home with a headache and she was never the slightest bit tempted by the smooth good looks and easy charm of Bernard or Laurent or Yves, nor by the quieter attractions of Guy or Marc.

In other areas of her life, the interconnected threads continued to play slowly out.

Walking past the Ransans' shop one evening on her way to a social gathering, she saw the 'For Sale' signs in the window, and in a letter home to her parents, she reported, 'Cousin Jeanne's health is deteriorating. Apparently…' according to Jacques, actually, but the word 'apparently' was safer '…she is not likely to last out the winter. I've got very fond of her, as it happens, and still can't understand why I wasn't even told of her existence before I came here!'

October gave way to November, and this time Sister Marie-Pierre really was cured when she was permitted to return to the convent. Just in case, though, she was given a strict schedule of follow-up appointments at Jacques's surgery, and would be reminded about each one in advance by the mechanical Madame Trimaille.

Madame Chaillet had now been on her terrible medication for just over eight weeks and was feeling better each day. Her kidney function was holding steady at its reduced level, and the system-wide impact of the fungus was losing its grip.

Her mouth ulcers had gone, there was no further gastric bleeding and her platelet and white cell counts were improving each time a blood sample was taken. The inflammation in her lymph glands was subsiding, her liver and spleen were returning to normal size and she had even put on a little weight, despite the drug's effect on her appetite.

Even her lungs, which had been the most obviously affected organ initially and which had given Jacques such trouble with their misleading appearance on X-ray, were getting much clearer.

'You see!' Remy Chapuis told Madame Chaillet condescendingly. 'We didn't kill you, after all! Once that diagnosis had been made, it was plain sailing, wasn't it?'

Isabelle glowered at him. She had had to call him in to restart Madame Chaillet's drip, as it had stopped flowing due to infiltration of the surrounding tissue. He looked haggard, and muttered that he'd been on call and up half the night, yet he seemed to perform the routine medical task very quickly, turning his back to both patient and nurse—which gave Madame Chaillet the opportunity to make a silly face. She was thoroughly familiar with the man by this time and impervious now to his brutal combination of tactlessness, ego and unfortunate wit.

Dr Chapuis left a moment later and Isabelle took a look at his handiwork. Untidy, and that bandage... Surely it wasn't the same one that he'd just taken off in order to reach the drip site? It certainly didn't look neat and snug enough to protect the vulnerable opening in the skin. Cursing the addition to her workload, she replaced the bandage with a new sterile dressing.

Plain sailing, Dr Chapuis had said! All those ravaging symptoms, all that uncertainty, and there had been days when Madame Chaillet's husband had teasingly proposed that his wife charge admission to her room. Had she done so, she really would have made a tidy sum from the number of medical students who were brought in to have a look at her.

She had borne all of this with good grace and, with any luck, it *would* all be plain sailing from now on.

Two DAYS LATER, Isabelle cursed this complacency. Madame Chaillet's drip site had become infected. Carine Faivre drew her attention to the fact after the night shift.

'Look at it. That's not right, is it? How could it have happened? Dr Ransan has been so strict about everyone using aseptic technique, and *not* using this IV line to take blood or infuse anything else.'

'Yes, but you know the junior doctors complain they don't have time to start a new line,' Isabelle pointed out. 'And Dr Chapuis the other day...'

She remembered his casual—not to say sloppy—replacing of the drip the other day and sat up straight. 'In fact, it was *definitely* him.' After she described the incident to the other nurse they both agreed that it was more than likely he was responsible.

'Not that that helps,' Carine said. 'The question is—what do we do about it? Tell the next doctor who drifts by, I suppose.'

'Provided it's *not* Dr Chapuis!'

It wasn't. It was Jacques, just minutes later, while Carine and Isabelle were still finishing up—standing just outside the door of the four-bed room next to Madame Chaillet's while Carine summarised the changes in the status of the other patients who would be under Isabelle's care over the next eight hours.

'Now, I'm tired,' she finished. '*You* can tell Dr Ransan about Madame Chaillet's drip site!'

It was not necessary. Having just seen the patient himself, he had discovered the problem already and was bearing angrily down upon them, his height intimidating and his movements angular.

Carine Faivre was quite a large and solid specimen of French womanhood, yet somehow he had eyes only for Isabelle, and began before he had even reached her. 'Are you aware that Madame Chaillet's drip site is infected? How has this been allowed to happen, after the strict orders I've given all along? You've known that the antifungal drug would not be effective against any bacteria there. Now we'll have to start her on antibiotics. Any additional drug is the last thing we need when this patient has already been through so much! I'm very disappointed in you, Mademoiselle Bonnet!'

For a moment, Isabelle verged on tears, then the pendulum swung back and she was overpowered by an anger quite as potent as his own. How dared he blame her? *Attack* her like this when Carine was standing right there, potentially just as culpable. How dared he even *exist*—nothing more than a thorn in her side, a gauntlet to run, a burden to bear? It would have been the blessing of her life if she'd never met the man! And the fact that she'd actually spent a night with him...!

Her hand lifted of its own accord, her palm flattened out hard, and her arm wound itself up with a powerful backthrust, then began its rapid arc towards his face, that tanned cheek invitingly defenceless. 'You judgemental, presumptuous—'

'What Isabelle means, Dr Ransan,' came in Carine firmly, attaching her fingers to Isabelle's wrist like a clamp and heading off the stinging slap with a scant two inches to spare, 'is that we were just about to tell you about Dr Chapuis's failure to use a sterile bandage on Wednesday. No doubt he simply forgot. He is overworked, as are we all—no one more than yourself, I expect—and we were about to ask for your directions as to treatment. Since you've just given us those, perhaps there's no more to be said?' she finished hopefully, as Isabelle's arm fell reluctantly to her side.

'No,' growled Jacques, 'I expect there isn't.'

He was still struggling, Isabelle saw. Perhaps it was merely the need for forbearance in front of two nurses with regard to Dr Chapuis, who was so universally disliked that it was becoming a bit of a scandal.

'Start with the antibiotic, then, Mademoiselle Bonnet, when I've written out the order, and we'll keep an eye on the situation,' he managed, then moved down the ward to his next patient.

Carine shrugged. 'He's not usually like that.'

'Neither am I!' muttered Isabelle.

'I'M NOT USUALLY like that,' Jacques said to her from the darkened corridor outside her little apartment at nine o'clock that night.

'Aren't you?' she answered tightly, after her first suppressed gulp of shock as she opened the door. 'I wouldn't really know, I'm afraid.'

'Isabelle...' he groaned, then contained himself. 'May I come in?'

'That depends— Oh, go ahead, yes.'

Sick of this pointless pretence that she didn't care, she stepped back. She felt the flowing skirt of the casual dress she wore over a white T-shirt stroking her thighs, blown by the small gust of air created by the open door. It was warm in here. Madame Claire controlled the central heating from her floor, and she liked a well-heated apartment.

Jacques was dressed for the crisp November night in grey pants and a chunky black sweater, topped by an equally solid grey leather jacket. He didn't remove it, though, just hunched his shoulders inside the garment and thrust his hands deep in its pockets, as if needing the confinement.

'This morning, I'm talking about, of course. The problem with Madame Chaillet's drip site.'

'Yes, I know.'

'Beyond that…' He began to pace, making her small *salon* seem, for the first time, claustrophobic. 'I don't know why I've come, except that this is becoming…impossible.'

'Yes, I know.'

'*Dieu*, Isabelle, if only you had been pregnant after that night!'

'*What?* My God, you arrogant, insensitive…' She spluttered to a halt.

'You are not ready for a child, obviously.' He kept pacing as he spoke, too restless to stay still, it seemed. 'And yet I was hoping for it more than anything, Isabelle, no matter how crazy that seems, and despite what you said about how unlikely it was. God, the disappointment—when I'd tricked myself into believing that it might have happened…!'

'*That* was what you meant about deceiving yourself on the subject of hornomes?' She was too bewildered to be angry now. So he hadn't meant that comment in the crass way she'd thought. What on earth *had* he meant? '*Why*, Jacques?'

'Don't you understand?' He spread his hands. 'It's the only thing that could have overridden what I owe my father. Had I started our child inside you, nothing could have stopped us from—'

He didn't finish, just came up and silently engulfed her in a kiss at once so tender and so demanding—so urgent and so complete—that she didn't even question her response, just gave it fully and honestly.

Arching upwards, she pulled his face down to hers,

cupped that warm, tanned and slightly raspy jaw between her hands then threaded her fingers back into his thick hair.

His glasses were not a problem. He took them off and threw them onto the soft, rounded back of the couch where they rested, immediately forgotten. He lifted her, tightening his arms around her, then set her down again to stroke her thighs. Pressing against him, Isabelle felt her breasts aching like tender buds with the throb of her heart beneath, and knew that his own pulses and breathing had quickened too.

It was too wonderful to stop. Just to be here, alone with him, in his arms and not questioning the fact—pushing aside all thoughts of anything but the sensation and emotion of it. She gave herself to him with every hungry movement of her lips, every touch of skin or yielding cloth, and when—after a long time—he tried to rein himself in and to push her away she would have none of it and only held him more closely and chased his retreating mouth with her own.

He gave up trying to resist and with a groan let his head descend to hers once more.

I love him, Isabelle thought.

It wasn't a sudden, thunder-struck revelation. Rather the knowledge came like a flood tide, swelling smoothly, rapidly and inexorably. At first she felt just the simple happiness and rightness of being here, of having him here—no longer angry with him, no longer mistrusting their night together. Then came the need to have this perfection continue. Finally, she just knew what it all meant.

It had been there from their first meeting—that feeling that there was a melody playing somewhere which she ought to recognise. It had been there in the passionate coupling of two people who should have seemed almost like strangers. It had been there in her hurt response to what she had seen as a callously male dismissal of their night together.

Its growth ought to have been stunted, frozen off by his insistence that it must not and could not happen, but instead it had continued...

Like a *thistle,* she thought rebelliously. No matter how you try to uproot it, it grows back all the stronger. Yes, very much like a thistle, and surely there was nothing romantic about that! It was painful and uncomfortable and unwanted.

They pulled apart at the same moment.

'This is terrible,' he groaned. 'I think I only wanted to come because of this. I told myself I needed to apologise, and I did. I wanted you so badly this morning, Isabelle, that wanting became anger and I attacked you when I had no reason to think it was your fault. "I'll apologise," I thought, and when I realised that the only way I could do it with our schedules today was by coming here tonight when I was sure that you would be alone I was so pleased...'

He groaned again.

'I saw the "For Sale" sign in your parents' shop window,' Isabelle said. It should have been a *non sequitur,* but it wasn't.

'Yes,' he answered. 'As we expected, the son has put it on the market straight away and wants the cash, not some long-term arrangement for a mortgage or a lease-purchase from my father. *Papa* is railing against his fate again, and your father's name has been invoked many times. He won't approach Jeanne.'

'Why not? That I can't understand.'

'He's too ashamed. He feels he didn't stick up for her years ago as he should have done, given my grandfather's very cruel favouritism. Isabelle...'

He seized her hands and she squeezed them feverishly. 'Yes, Jacques?'

'We could embark on an affair—keep this secret from

my parents, and even from Claire if we managed it carefully.'

'Is that what you want? I would...I will... I—I want to be with you, Jacques!'

'Yes, and I feel the same. It's... Well, before we met I'd started to wonder what I was waiting for and why I had always held back with the women in my life. The day— very possibly the *minute*—I saw you trapped in that ridiculous store-room by our dear Dr Chapuis, I suddenly knew.'

'Yes... Just to be together. I *will* do it, Jacques.'

'No,' he groaned. 'I can't ask it of you.'

'Why not?'

'Because I won't, that's all. It would be all the things I *don't* want in a relationship between us. Secrecy and dishonesty, snatched time together, and always the knowledge that I was betraying my father and that if he found out it would undoubtedly crush and twist him to the point where he would become impossible to live with. My mother puts up with so much already... Soon you would want far more than a hole-and-corner affair, and I would want to give it to you. We would start to hate each other...'

'No!'

'Yes, Isabelle! We're both very passionate people. You're volatile, while I have—'

'Those depths that run beneath still waters,' she conceded.

'And hate could take root so quickly amongst all of that. Love under constraint is fertile ground for hate, Isabelle, and I can't stand even the thought of fighting and sniping at you—of bitterness or regret between us. I've hated your anger lately. I've been angry myself. I couldn't bear those cords of emotion to thicken and strangle everything that was good between us.'

She moved away from him, clutching her arms across her

front—painfully, achingly disappointed. Her little laugh was very shallow. 'I thought at first you were asking me to throw myself onto the bed for your love-making here and now.'

He groaned, then laughed harshly. 'I was. I wanted to! I still want to! But…haven't I just convinced both of us that I mustn't?'

'I—I suppose so. Yes. Yes, you have. I can't stand the thought of hating you either.'

'I must go, then.'

'Yes, or else we'll—'

They looked at each other. He looked tortured, his hair in wild disarray and his brown eyes naked and fiercely stormy. Pained and vulnerable, too, which made her heart twist. Such a capable man… She was probably in much the same state. He began to move towards the door, his assured bearing belying the heightened emotion that still bounced off the walls.

'Jacques?'

'Yes?'

'Don't forget your glasses.'

She picked them up and went to give them to him and their fingers touched, clinging together for a moment in one futile gesture of connection. Then he put the tortoiseshell frames back onto the bridge of his nose and they smiled briefly at each other.

'Can you see me when you're not wearing those?' she asked idly, to fill the remaining space in his journey to the door.

'See you, yes. But you're a blur, and your hair is a halo—like a dark angel in the mist,' he said.

He reached the door and left, and only once he had gone did she realise that neither of them had bothered to say goodbye.

'NOTHING PLANNED WITH your student friends for this evening?' Madame Claire asked over a breakfast of coffee and croissants the next morning.

She had invited Isabelle down, as she often did on a Saturday, since Isabelle had the weekends off.

'Anny said I should drop by the Café Renoir. She's not counting on me at all, though. Why?'

'There is a party, and I promised I would get you to come if I could. There will be people of all ages, not just boring old things like myself.'

'Well, leaving aside the fact that you're the most inter-esting person I know, Madame Claire, I'd love to come.' The enthusiasm she squeezed into her voice was an effort. Nothing seemed rosy today.

'Excellent!' Claire replied. 'It will be somewhat formal, at the château of the Chavin-Joissy winery, south of here, near Arbois. I have known the Joissy family for years. We'll order a taxi, and collect Jeanne on the way. Do wear your very *best*...'

Isabelle grimaced. 'Not sure that even my *very* best is good enough for the...what is it?'

'Château Chavin-Joissy, but it's only a *small* château, Isabelle.'

'Still... You've seen the outfit. Silky pants and top, in a sort of peacockish turquoise.'

'Not a dress?'

'Not one for evening, I'm afraid.'

'Then do you know what I'm going to do?' Claire clapped her hands together. 'I'm going to get something from Jeanne. She has kept a few dozen of her original mod-els in perfect condition, and a really good couture dress like that doesn't date. Will you let me?'

Her eagerness was endearing, and Isabelle soon agreed to the plan. There seemed no reason not to. Claire would phone over Isabelle's measurements, Jeanne would find something to fit—'You're rather petite, but in the sixties models were not so leggy as they are nowadays'—and Isabelle would put it on when they went to pick up Jeanne.

The latter was waiting for them when they arrived at seven-thirty but she wore only a flowing silk kimono of vivid red and looked so ill, despite her inextinguishable beauty, that Isabelle was very worried. She forgot about the dress she was to exchange for her casual pants and top, and forgot about the taxi whose meter was ticking extravagantly in the street below.

'You should be in hospital, Cousin Jeanne.'

'No…' She waved her hand. 'I'm a little congested. Yes, it's…making my breathing worse, but I've been taking my medicine. I'll just stay home. I…have the dress for you. One of my very favourites. So lovely to see it worn again. Claire—'

Too breathless to speak more, she lay on the couch where pillows already rested to support her back, and Claire led the way into a spare bedroom where a shantung silk shift in a very dark red, with bag and shoes to match, reposed on a hanger. It fitted perfectly, and was so beautifully cut and styled, with its slightly off-the-shoulder neckline and figure-hugging darts at the waist, that Isabelle gasped at the sight of herself in the mirror—halo of tumbling dark hair flashing with golden lights, brown eyes, pale olive skin…

'But I don't understand how even the *shoes*…'

Claire dismissed the problem. 'A present from me. I sneaked a look at your size and phoned my favourite boutique. They had them sent up here.'

When Isabelle was ready they came back out to find Jeanne still on the couch, her breathing even worse. Despite the diuretics she was taking her feet and hands were swollen and slightly bluish.

'Exquisite!' she said of Isabelle's appearance, clapping her hands together.

'I hate seeing you…*leaving* you like this,' Isabelle said,

but Jeanne refused to accept any offer to cancel the evening and sit with her, or to admit her to hospital.

'Not yet,' she said. 'Give me a few more days at home, please.'

Claire and Isabelle exchanged an emotional look, then Claire bent and held Jeanne awkwardly for a long moment. On the way down to the waiting taxi she had to get out her lace handkerchief, and muttered crossly, 'This is so foolish! I'll smudge my make-up. Why can't crying be a prettier process?'

Isabelle took her trembling hand, not fooled for a second by the apparent triviality of her complaint. She knew that Claire would break down completely if she couldn't keep emotion at bay by twittering about her make-up.

'Oh, Madame Claire…'

'Don't! Don't! I'm not going to think of it all now. My dear, did you bring your mascara with you? I'm going to need to make some repairs…'

'No, I didn't bring it, and I'm going to need it, too, any second!'

'Jeanne would be horrified. She's always so perfectly groomed.'

'She is, isn't she? Quite gorgeous!'

'What is that North American animal that you have? The one they make caps out of?'

'A raccoon?'

'That's the one, and I am looking more like it every minute.'

They were both crying and laughing at the same time.

'There! We're coming beneath a streetlamp,' Claire said. 'Can you look at my eyes and tell me…?'

'Not nearly as bad as you'd think. No one will know.'

Fortunately they had half an hour to collect themselves and put their grief for Jeanne aside temporarily.

The Château Chavin-Joissy was, as Claire had said, a

modest one as châteaux went. Nonetheless, it was an old
and lovely building of a stone that looked as yellow as
honeycomb under the carefully placed golden floodlights
which illuminated it this evening. The affair was already in
full swing and Claire and Isabelle clung together a little at
first, not quite in a party mood.

They had to explain to Monsieur and Madame Joissy that
Jeanne had been too ill to come, and this brought a crowd-
ing response of concern and sympathy from many other
people so that it was quite some time before Isabelle was
able to acquire enough space to scan the room.

At which point she suddenly understood why Claire had
made such a fuss about getting her so beautifully dressed.
Jacques was here. Claire had seen him too, across the large
salon, where he stood at a long table helping himself to a
canapé, with a champagne flute already in his hand. If
Isabelle had still been in any doubt, the glint in the older
woman's eye would have proved her case.

'Claire…?'

'Do you think I haven't seen how you've been pining
for him? You're right for each other. *You* both know it, and
it's wrong to let another generation of Ransans and Bonnets
get in your way.'

'Will you please let Jacques and me make that decision
for ourselves?'

'Well, I would if I could trust you to make the right one,'
Claire retorted. 'But from what I've seen and heard, and
not seen and heard—'

'For heaven's sake,' Isabelle muttered, 'it's like conducting my emotional life in a test tube, with fourteen sci-
entists watching and taking notes!'

Jacques had seen her now too…or else it was just clumsiness that had made him drop both canapé and champagne
glass onto a snowy pile of table napkins, soaking most of
them. Of course it wasn't clumsiness! He hadn't expected

her here tonight and it had come as a shock, just as it had to Isabelle.

He looked fabulous in a black dinner suit with his hair brushed back from his high temples to strengthen that aura of intellect and authority, which was then immediately tempered by the humour around his mouth and, at the moment, a distinctly hunted expression. He quickly downed the soggy canapé and began to mop up the champagne, but a hired waiter soon shooed him away.

Claire, the witch, had somehow melted away completely... No, there she was, apparently completely embroiled in giving her opinion of President Chirac and smoking elegantly, although how she had got so far across the room and so deeply into serious conversation in what felt like about ten seconds Isabelle couldn't pause to wonder.

Jacques was here, looming over her, and he came straight to the point. 'Claire brought you?'

'Of course,' she answered bitterly.

'She doesn't trust anyone else's organisational capabilities, does she?'

'Apparently not!'

'If it would do any good for us to be in the same room together, Isabelle, believe me I'd make it happen. Daily!'

'I know.'

'So if I spend most of this evening *not* in the same room with you—*mon Dieu,* in that dress you look...' His voice came to a husky halt. 'You'll understand, won't you?'

'Of course. I think I always do, don't I? That's—'

'Part of the problem,' he agreed.

'Jeanne was supposed to come,' she told him now, 'but she felt too ill. Jacques, she's fighting it, but I think she needs to be admitted again. Could you perhaps pay a personal call over the next few days and see what you can do?'

'Of course. I went last week. I thought she'd last a little longer. What's happened?'

'She's congested. A cold, I think, that's gone onto her chest.'

'Damn! That's all it will take. I'll go tomorrow. Is that why Claire is so shrill and twittery tonight?'

'I think so. She loves all of you—all of *us,* really—so much, which is why she thinks she can do things like *this!*' She glowered at him and saw his hunted expression once again. It was cold comfort that they were *both* feeling miserable!

She realised how close they were standing and how intensely they were focused on each other only when a black-haired young woman in her early twenties with a large mouth, plastered at the moment with a large pout, joggled his elbow and complained, 'Jacques, I've been trying to get your attention for five minutes!'

'I'm sorry, Sabine,' he answered reluctantly.

'You know *Papa* wanted me to show you the remodelling we've done in the upstairs rooms. We're going to open three of them as exclusive guest quarters for foreign tourists. Not that business isn't good with our wines, but one can always…'

Her voice blended back into the general buzz of conversation as she steered him firmly away, and Isabelle watched that distinctive head bob above the throng until the pair of them disappeared through a distant door. She barely glimpsed him again for the rest of the evening.

That is, until Claire started making noises about going home.

'Jacques will take us,' she announced confidently, then looked about for him but couldn't find him.

Isabelle could have told her. He was over by that huge draped green velvet curtain, still in captured orbit around the pouting Mademoiselle Joissy and her *Papa,* who—even from this distance—was clearly doing everything he could to grease the wheels of romance.

I might as well wish him every success, too, Isabelle realised, since it doesn't make any difference to me. Is it just totally selfish of me, then, to be pleased that Jacques looks as miserable as I feel?

'Ah!' said Claire, having seen him now as well.

She towed Isabelle over, like a tugboat towing a barge, and told Monsieur Joissy quite brazenly, 'Hélène was looking for you, Jean-Pierre. You too, Sabine.' Then she said to Jacques, once her host and his daughter were out of earshot, equally brazenly, 'You don't look very happy, Jacques. Are you ready to leave, as we are?'

'No, Claire,' he answered with weary firmness, cutting straight to the heart of the matter. 'I will *not* take you and Isabelle home. The Duchesnes will be happy to, I'm sure. Yes, look, they're saying their goodbyes now. I appreciate that your intentions are only the very best, *ma chère Madame*, but, as Isabelle herself understands and will tell you, there are times when the happy ending that our hearts crave has to give way to the reality that love is only the beginning of a relationship, and that what comes afterwards can turn very sour.'

'Jacques? Jacques!' It was Sabine Joissy again, and he turned to her quickly with evident relief.

'Let's ask the Duchesnes, Madame Claire,' Isabelle begged quietly. 'My head is pounding, and perhaps I ate too much...'

'You didn't eat a thing!'

'...because I don't think this dress fits me all that well after all!'

CHAPTER TEN

JEANNE was admitted to the Hôpital Saint-Jean the next day.

Jacques knocked on Isabelle's door at ten o'clock to give her the news. She had slept late, after lying awake for what felt like hours following the party, and wasn't yet dressed so that she greeted him with wildly tousled hair and wearing only a fine cotton nightdress topped by a heavy patchwork dressing-gown made of dark-coloured velours and satins which was closely belted around her.

He told her the news about Jeanne as he stood in the doorway, giving only the brief fact of it and none of the details.

Needing to hear more, she urged him to come in, and only after he'd nodded briefly and ducked into her sunny little *salon* did she decide that perhaps it had been very foolish to extend the invitation.

He was casually but very attractively dressed in oatmeal-coloured pants and a dark green cable-knit sweater, and she asked, 'You did an early round at the hospital?'

'Yes, and went to Tante Jeanne's afterwards.'

'You found her worse, then?'

'Exhausted from the effort of breathing. She'd hardly slept. Frightened, I think, on top of the physical part of it.'

'Did she protest?'

'About being admitted? No.'

'We shouldn't have listened to her last night. We shouldn't have left her.'

'She expected that reaction from you, which was why she urged me to come and tell you straight away—you and Claire—that you're *not* to feel that.'

'Claire…'

'I've already told her. She's on her way to see Jeanne now. I expect you'll want to go as well, but leave it for a bit, hey? She needs to rest. Claire will see to it that she does, but if you were there she might feel compelled to make more of an effort. I've increased her diuretic and prescribed something for the chest congestion. It won't do much…'

'Heart ward again?'

'No, your ward, actually. She's more familiar with it, and she knows that you'll be there during the week. She asked if she could be there and there's no reason why not since there's so little we can do for either her heart or her lungs.'

'Thanks for telling me, Jacques,' she said.

'Am I dismissed, then?'

She looked at him and sighed. 'Only if you want to be.'

'You know I don't…and you know I *should.*'

'Oh, just *stay,* Jacques! Let's at least… I *like* you, for heaven's sake, on top of everything else that's so impossible. Couldn't we sit here and watch the sun on the rooftops and eat croissants? Did you have breakfast before you rounded?'

'No, I didn't…'

'Then I'll squeeze orange juice and make coffee and a full Canadian breakfast for you, shall I, as well as the croissants? Eggs and ham and home-fried potatoes. If you'll go to the bakery for me while I get dressed…'

'I rather like you in that,' he grinned.

'Let's not make this *too* hard, please!'

'No,' he agreed soberly, 'let's not. It's impossibly hard already.'

'It is,' she agreed grimly. 'Now go to the bakery!'

He let himself out and she went into the bedroom, thinking, I keep hoping something's going to change. But what? There's a key somewhere, a crisis that's building. I *feel* it, but I can't think what it can be. We can't go on like this, pretending that we're not seeing each other—not involved. Holding ourselves back and yet secretly—fooling ourselves about it—digging ourselves in deeper. It was easier when I thought I had reason to be angry with him.

Now… Every new little thing I get to know about him… Silly things, some of them! Watching him eat that ruined canapé while he mopped up his champagne last night; getting to recognise that merciless politeness of his when he chews someone out for a mistake; his deceptive vagueness when he's thinking hard about something, and his total focus when his feelings are involved.

'I've only known him…what…two months, and yet every new thing I find out just *fits* and right now I'm filling up and floating like a helium balloon just because we're about to have *breakfast!*

She showered in two minutes flat, then put on camel-coloured jodhpur-cut pants and a figure-hugging black angora sweater and bundled her hair high into a ponytail with a stretchy black ribbon. Then she squeezed oranges and put on coffee and was just dicing onion and potato very finely for the home fries when he returned, enveloped in the aura of still-warm croissants and wielding a long *parisien* loaf like a weapon.

'Can I help?' he asked.

'No,' she told him firmly. 'This is my treat. You can…I don't know…sit and entertain me with your scintillating conversation. How was your round this morning? Any news?'

There was, as it happened. Firstly, Madame Chaillet's infection from her drip site was already much improved, which was definitely good news. And, secondly, Gerard

Perrin, the old cheese-maker from Crozelay, had been admitted to the men's medical ward yesterday, after panicking at the sight of blood in his sputum.

'All indications are that he's just stripped his throat lining,' Jacques explained. 'He'd been away for a week, visiting his brother, and had been smoking more heavily than usual. We'll do a bronchoscopy but his X-ray was pretty clear, despite his evident chronic bronchitis. He couldn't believe it. He'd already buried himself, I think—or at least decided on the hymns for his funeral—and was cursing himself for not taking my advice and coming in a month ago.'

'Will he stop smoking?'

Jacques made a helpless gesture. 'He has. For the moment. Who knows? Madame Claire hasn't, for all she professes to think me the most marvellous doctor who ever lived. She listens to my little lecture on the subject in the winter when her bronchitis gets quite bad, then goes away again with her sugar-coated stubbornness utterly intact.'

Isabelle echoed his wry laugh, and served their breakfast. *Brunch* really, as it was almost eleven. The sun came brightly through the window where the small table stood, etching his profile with light, and she was so aware of him that she was almost dizzy with it.

They ate and talked and refilled their coffee-cups twice, and soon it was twelve. At which point, glancing at his watch, he moved restlessly and frowned, then said gloomily and belligerently, 'It's a gorgeous day, you know, not like November at all.'

'Yes, I've noticed.'

'And you haven't even been out yet,' he accused.

'I haven't had a chance.'

'True, but it would be a crime to waste the day.'

'Oh, definitely.'

'So I really think I'd better take you somewhere.'

'Like…?'

'Like the Châ de Joux, or the source of the River Loue.'
He stood up as she began to clear their dishes away, and
came to take them firmly out of her hands. 'Don't bother
with that.'

'You want to leave straight away?'

'I think we'd better,' he growled, 'or we won't manage
to go anywhere at all.'

They looked at each other, and the slow heat simmering
between them suddenly burst into the inevitable flame. He
scooped her into his arms, strode towards the two doors,
each just ajar, on the far side of the room and muttered,
'Which is the bedroom?'

'This one…'

He kicked the door open, flung her onto the bed and
rasped, 'Can I do this, Isabelle? Can I make love to you
again? And maybe this time the child that I ached to start
inside you…'

'Oh, yes, maybe…'

'Why are we fooling ourselves like this?'

'I—I don't care.'

'Neither do I.'

He slid his body down beside hers, pulled her to him
once more and kissed her fiercely and briefly.

'Oh, please, yes…!' she murmured as his lips trailed
away. He rolled from the bed and onto his feet, and she sat
up slowly, her head swimming and heart pounding.

She hadn't known that a man could strip so grace-
fully…or so quickly. In half a minute he was standing
there, tall and brown and magnificent, while she was still
seated on the edge of the bed and fumbling with the buttons
at the sides of her trousers.

'Let me help,' he entreated somewhat hoarsely, pulling
her to her feet, but he was too impatient and that got in the

way so she had to finish after all, laughing because without his 'help' she would have been done a good minute sooner.

The black sweater, though, was a different story. He peeled it expertly upwards then dived hungrily at her breasts, nuzzling them with his mouth as he unclipped her bra at the back then let it slide between them so that her slight, silky-skinned breasts were pressed against the warmth of his chest.

Then, at last, they were entwined together skin to skin. They fell to the bed again and she felt his warm contours mapped against her skin, felt the blood pulsing in him. Her breathing was high and shallow, and this was totally overpowering.

For a long time he just gazed at her, stroking with a hypnotic rhythm the shallow S-shape that curved from her breast to her hip as she lay on her side. Then he moved the necessary inch to reach her lips and captured her mouth in a kiss as deliberate and sensual as eating a peach.

That flame ignited again, and she closed her eyes and lost herself completely to physical sensation—taste and touch and sound and smell, the moist warm friction of heated skin on skin, the rhythm of movement on top of the insistent pulses that ran beneath.

He used words more sensuously than she had known was possible—in French—a kind of love poetry that named each part of her body and what it did to him. She was too heart-full to reply, except with laughter and cat-like growls deep in her throat.

Afterwards, she couldn't have explained or described or even quite *remembered* just what it had been about his touch and hers—just where or how or what—but somehow they had come together in a shattering explosion of sensuality, where giving and receiving had become indistinguishable, and the very boundaries of their two bodies were blurred.

As the frenzied tide ebbed, he held her against his chest and folded her quilt over the two of them so that they lay in a downy cocoon, with the sun slanting in at an angle which just reached to the edge of the bed. It meant that the zenith of the day was already past, and she watched the progress of the sun into the room drowsily for a few minutes until they both dozed.

He was the first to awaken, and when she opened her own eyes she saw him looking at her lazily, his long lashes almost tangled together. Bathed in the unrelenting heat of this regard, she murmured confusedly, 'So, what's the matter? Did my face turn blue?'

'No…'

'Well, then, I guess I should just take it as a compliment, or something.'

'Please do…'

'You're still staring.'

He sighed. 'Just lost…in you…and trying not to get found.'

'Get found?'

'There's a search party,' he explained, half teasing, half serious. 'A whole squadron—maybe a battalion—of very serious, rigid thoughts out to hunt this euphoria I'm feeling and shoot it down, and I'm determined that the euphoria is going to escape unscathed. In fact—'

Suddenly he was restless, and flung the quilt aside. 'Let's make a break for it while we still can.'

'Jacques? What—?'

'Oh, I don't know, Isabelle.' He was pacing now, catching up his compact navy briefs then kicking his legs impatiently into his trousers. With torso still bare, he said, 'Yes, I do! This is everything we've said—'

'Couldn't happen.'

'*Mustn't* happen! But it has and I— Well, I'm revising my opinion of Romeo. Hell! What is it about you? I never thought I'd reach the point where resistance...just wasn't *possible!*'

She said nothing for a minute, groping, then burst out, 'I suppose I don't even want to think about it.'

'Let's go out. Let me take you somewhere.'

So they dressed and got in his car and drove up along the road that led to the Swiss border, where the ancient Château de Joux perched grimly above the pass through the mountains. They took the guided tour and heard the elaborate commentary on the dungeon of Berthe de Joux and the two hundred and twelve steps around the old well, and it was a charming and completely meaningless afternoon, with them behaving like friends but feeling like lovers, or— at inevitable, tumultuous times—behaving like lovers but not knowing if, tomorrow, they'd still feel justified in even speaking to each other.

The autumn sun began to fade early and it was soon chilly so they took the journey back, winding along less-travelled routes until after dark and then stopping on impulse at a restaurant in a small village and eating *fondue Savoyarde.*

He stayed the night in her apartment. On the floor below, Claire's windows were darkened, and after Jacques had phoned the hospital he confirmed, 'She's spending the night with Jeanne. I'll allow more visitors tomorrow. My father will want to go.'

'You mean the end is that close?'

'It's possible. Or she may pull through this and have a few more weeks, a couple of months. But why wait? Jeanne herself seems to bear him no grudge. I can't quite work out what it is between those two. There seems to be guilt on both sides. I'd like to get them together and force the issue. My God, I'd like to get your parents here! Bring everyone together and let all the skeletons come rattling out of the cupboard so that maybe—'

He didn't need to finish, and when they made love an hour later, there was an added ingredient of urgency—like the way people made love for the very last time before being parted by war—that made the mix *too* potent somehow.

Isabelle woke the next morning at six and prepared herself for work, feeling as groggy and heavy as if she'd been drugged.

Jacques, needing to get to his apartment to change before rounds, had already gone.

He must have phoned his parents during the brief stopover at his place. Or perhaps Claire, who was still keeping vigil beside her friend, had taken a typical hand in the matter. Whatever the case, François and Giselle Ransan arrived at eleven forty-five.

Isabelle was not nursing Jeanne. She had explained privately to Simone Boucher that there was a distant family connection, and that it might be better if someone else was assigned to her care.

'Alix will do a good job with her,' was Simone Boucher's response. 'She's more sensitive than you would think, that one, despite her flirtatious ways. She lost her mother to cancer three years ago, you know.'

'I didn't know, actually,' Isabelle said, 'but I like Alix.'

So Isabelle was at the nurses' station, adding some notes to Madame Chaillet's voluminous chart, when her father's cousin and his wife came into the ward. They saw her and approached, and she was just about to point them in the direction of Jeanne's room when Madame Ransan asked, sounding agitated, 'Jacques is not here, is he?'

'No, he has appointments this morning,' Isabelle told them.

'Of course! How stupid of me! I was counting on seeing him here. I didn't think at all! The shop has been sold and I wanted—'

'Sold?' She knew at once what this would mean to them.

'Yes. We got the news just an hour ago,' Giselle confirmed.

François had headed in the direction of the visitors' bathroom, and Isabelle turned instinctively to watch him.

Following her gaze, Giselle Ransan said, 'I had to drag him here. Oh, I'm burdening you with all this again, *mademoiselle,* but you are a friend of my son's and of Madame Claire... Jeanne has been such a success. He loves *and* hates her for it. They rarely see each other, the two of them, but he's her twin...'

'Yes, they look alike. Both so intense and alive. Like Jacques, and yet his colouring is so different.'

'If only François hadn't been too proud to ask for her help... May I phone Jacques? Perhaps he can come as soon as his appointments are finished. I need him here!'

She made the call, then François emerged from the bathroom. Giselle seized his arm as if still afraid he would leave, and they went to see Jeanne together. She was in a private room at the end of the corridor, and Isabelle very much wanted to be there now, but she knew she must not. She'd dropped in briefly first thing this morning with Jacques—and that had been hard, disguising the new electricity between them from Claire—to sit quietly with Jeanne for ten minutes, neither of them speaking more than a few words.

But now she had her own patients to deal with, none of them seriously ill. Perhaps at lunchtime... She was due for her break at noon.

Noon, when Jacques's hours ended for the morning.

He came in at ten past twelve, when she was just ready to go off, knowing that she needed to eat to fuel herself for the afternoon after only a light breakfast six hours ago, but feeling the pull towards Jeanne's room.

Jacques made the decision for her. 'Come!'

'I—'

'I need you, Isabelle.'

And that was all it took, of course. Their eyes met and she saw the painful ambivalence of her own feelings mirrored in his. Their situation hadn't changed. It had only got harder, with the pull stronger now in both directions. The selling of the shop would make François's regrets about his life even stronger, and yesterday had added a strand of steel to the tightly twisted bond between herself and Jacques. She felt incurably joined to him now.

In the room at the end of the corridor Claire was making her familiar plea. 'Don't tire yourself by talking, Jeanne, dear!' Madame Oudot's cheeks were pink, her eyes bright and glittering and her hands twisted together anxiously. 'Now is not the time to—'

'It is,' Jeanne rasped. 'It *is!*'

'No! After all these years, what good can it do? Hold onto everything you've won so dearly, Jeanne. Please!'

'Claire?' Isabelle went up to her, concerned. She must have barely slept, sitting there all night in that rigid chair beside Jeanne's bed. She looked drained and distraught and, despite her sprightly manner and zest for life, her own health was not perfect.

'Oh, Isabelle, Isabelle!'

'What is it, Madame Claire?'

'Everything I've done for this family, every piece of advice I've given and caution I've made and secret I've kept has been for the best, you know, and with the best intentions, the best love in the world. Jeanne and François could almost have been my children...'

'I know,' Isabelle soothed. 'I know. And *they* know it, too, Madame Claire. Don't upset yourself about it now. Jeanne knows just why you're here by her bed, just how much you love her.'

'But she's bought François's shop for him, you see, and—'

'What?' Jacques came in. 'But, *Maman,* you and *Papa* wouldn't let me ask her about it. You wouldn't even let me tell her it was to be sold. Did you change your mind without telling me? No! Then who—?'

'I told Jeanne, of course,' Claire said. 'And she set her lawyer and her bank manager onto it at once, as I knew she would. It is to be a gift to François and Giselle, naturally.'

'But why?' François spoke, and only now did Isabelle get a chance to observe the sudden change in him. There was a weight lifted from his shoulders, and a suggestion of his strength had returned. But he was puzzled, too, and uneasy—as was everyone.

There was something about Claire's agitation, and Jeanne's need to speak...

'Because...it was...I, François.' The effort was immense, and her struggle for breathing painful to watch.

Isabelle saw that, despite the increased use of diuretics, Jeanne's feet and lower legs, as well as the hands that worked on the sheet in front of her, were badly swollen, and there was no position in the hospital bed that could give her misshapen spine any comfort. Her face had a strength and beauty, though, as she pressed on with desperate urgency, 'I who...took that wretched money...of *Papa's.*'

'You?'

'Yes. Claire—tell it!'

'You!' François repeated. 'Madame Claire?'

'Yes, yes. It's out now! It was Jeanne who took it, and it was *I* who kept it all a secret. The two of you—you, François, and your father, Isabelle—had been heard often enough threatening to rob Charles of that well-known stash of his.'

'But Jeanne had already run away to Paris when it disappeared.'

'She came back. She saw after two days that it was useless to be there if she didn't have money so she took it, then came to me, stricken by conscience and wanting to put it back. "Why?" I asked her. "It's the *only* use your father will ever have been to you!" I was with Felix by this time, of course, and I had no illusions left about what Charles Ransan was. And as for who would be blamed, I rightly foresaw that Raoul would suspect François and François would suspect Raoul, which left Jeanne free to pursue her only chance of success.

'I told your mother the truth, Isabelle, and told her to throw herself on your father and make him take her to Canada, and I told *you,* François, that Giselle had loved you since she was twelve and that you were a fool if you didn't love her back—which you soon found that you did! So I was right on all counts. The only thing I did *not* foresee—and I should have done—was that Charles would insist on suspecting François, despite Raoul's very guilty-looking flight.'

'And you let that happen, Madame Claire,' Jacques came in slowly and ominously, breaking the stunned silence after a moment. 'You *let* my father's medical career go to the dogs to shield Jeanne! *Papa*...'

He turned to his father, his eyes blazing, but François Ransan had his palms pressed against his eyes.

Claire spoke softly, going up to the big man and laying her small jewelled fingers on his massive arm. 'Isn't it time you admitted the truth to yourself, François, my dear, now that you don't have a convenient cousin thousands of miles away to blame for your life? Are you really going to switch your bitterness to Jeanne, your own sister?

'Tell your son about that summer of 1960. Your medical studies were already finished, weren't they? You'd done so poorly in your exams that you had been asked to leave. You were bright enough, it was said, but the attractions of Paris had been too strong and you hadn't worked. Charles had kept such a tight rein on you that when you went away it snapped and you went wild, despite the two women you had waiting for you here.'

'Is this true, *Papa?*' Jacques demanded. 'Is all of this true?'

'Yes, it's true,' François growled. 'If I had taken certain subjects over again, there would have been a chance, and I told myself that I would have taken them and succeeded if Papa had been prepared to pay but, if I'm honest…' He paused, having to struggle to make the admission. 'No. I would not have studied as I needed to. I can see that now. I don't have the patience and commitment that you do, Jacques. It has been…easy to blame Raoul Bonnet all these years but, no, Madame Claire is right. I won't switch my blame now to Jeanne.'

He went up to his sister and touched her sunken shoulder. 'Can you ever forgive me, Jeanne, for not knocking our father down with my fists for the things he said to you at times?'

'Of course, François. So long ago! Sit with me now?'

'Jeanne?' Claire stepped forward anxiously.

'Don't worry. Not dying today after all,' she joked with effort. 'Maybe tomorrow. Or next week. Want to enjoy this first.'

In the room there was a feeling something like that of the aftermath to deafening fireworks—a silence so loud that ears rang and every sound was muffled and the echoes of light-bursts still flickered before the eyes. Giselle was holding onto a still-flustered Claire, Jeanne was smiling wryly at François, while Jacques and Isabelle…

'If I spoke to Madame Boucher,' he murmured to her, 'do you think there's any chance I'd be able to take you for a long lunch? I don't have appointments again until two.'

'I suppose I'm owed a long lunch, really,' she answered him dazedly. 'Simone has been promising me a bit of make-up time for about three weeks now for breaks I've missed.'

They left the ward five minutes later, took the lift in silence and arrived at his car, still without saying a word. It simply wasn't necessary. Everything was already clear and perfectly understood between them. There was a faint, familiar melody in the air somewhere suddenly, and Isabelle knew what it was at last…the bells of the Église Saint-Paul, tolling for a wedding.

'Where to go, that's the question,' Jacques muttered to himself as he began to drive.

'Your place?' she suggested tentatively. 'Last time I was there I…had a wonderful time.'

'Seems a long time ago.'

'It does! Now…'

'All the cards are on the table, and there are rather *more* of them than I'd thought.'

'Than anyone thought. And it seems that Claire was holding them all.'

'Did you check her sleeves?' he asked. 'I'd hardly be surprised to see several more aces and kings come tumbling out.'

'All trumps, of course,' she suggested.

'Of course!'

'She's definitely the villain of the piece, isn't she?' Isabelle said. 'Advising everyone, protecting everyone from themselves. I suppose this is why I never heard anything about Jeanne from my parents. She was kept secret, along with the money she stole. But why didn't Claire say anything sooner?'

'Because for a long time it didn't matter,' Jacques

pointed out. 'Who would have benefited from knowing the truth? Your parents, who evidently *did* know, have their own lives in Canada, successful from what you've said. My father knew the most important truth all along, which was that he'd scuttled that medical career of his all on his own—only he refused to acknowledge the fact. And who knows? Perhaps it was his regret that drove me to success. Claire would claim that, I suspect.'

'The witch! I love her still, you know.'

'I know!'

'And the truth about that money…'

'Only started to matter again when you and I began to love each other.'

'By which point the secret had got to be such a habit with Claire that she couldn't see it was time to give it up. Like her nicotine!'

'And she was still protecting Jeanne, of course. She was afraid that that theft still wouldn't be forgiven, but I think the gift of the shop will cancel that out.'

'And Jeanne's illness,' Isabelle added.

They reached his apartment, and he parked his car so hurriedly that the front bumper grated badly on the stone wall.

He shrugged, and Isabelle laughed. 'I've never liked men who cared too much about their cars!'

'Good,' he responded, 'because I can think of at least fifty things that would come higher on my list, and most of them have something to do with you.'

He didn't wait to reach the privacy of his apartment— just pulled her into his arms there and then on the stone steps that led up to his door, bending to her with a kiss that had her breathless and melting within seconds. She wrapped her arms around him and arched upwards, then carefully plucked those difficult glasses from his nose, folded them and placed them in the breast pocket of her uniform before something disastrous could happen.

Long minutes later he attempted to prove that he could get out his keys and open his front door while still kissing her more thoroughly than she'd ever been kissed in her life but, alas, he couldn't achieve this feat of dexterity, and the sound of another apartment's window opening somewhere above their heads forced him to concentrate on the less satisfying of the two tasks. His keys…

Inside, their shared urgency lessened a little. 'Do you realise that we don't have to be heroic about this any more?' he whispered against her ear.

'Yes…'

'Although I must confess I had begun to rehearse certain speeches to my father about conquering the past, forgiving one's enemies and looking to the welfare of future generations.'

'Had you?'

He pulled away from her and was suddenly much more serious. 'I was truly torn, Isabelle. Our sense of family is, I think, very strong here in France.'

'I like that. I'm looking forward to getting to know your family, Jacques. Your mother seems wonderful, and even your father. Your sisters, too.'

'They'll love you. Thérèse phoned me the other day and asked some rather suspicious questions about you. I'm sure Claudine will have heard rumours already.'

'All we have to do is tell Claire, and everyone she's ever met will hear not only rumours but every last detail!'

'Then let's keep it to ourselves for a few days, shall we? Enjoy the freedom to love and discover each other that we should have had all along…'

'Just a few days?' she asked, half teasing, half wistful.

'As long as you like,' he promised, grazing her mouth

with his. 'Now that we've no reason to keep this a secret, it might be distinctly pleasurable to do just that...'

'In that case,' she murmured wickedly, 'what a pity this is only lunch!'

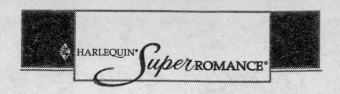

HARLEQUIN Presents

**The world's bestselling romance series...
The series that brings you your favorite authors,
month after month:**

Helen Bianchin...Emma Darcy
Lynne Graham...Penny Jordan
Miranda Lee...Sandra Marton
Anne Mather...Carole Mortimer
Susan Napier...Michelle Reid

and many more uniquely talented authors!

Wealthy, powerful, gorgeous men...
Women who have feelings just like your own...
The stories you love, set in exotic, glamorous locations...

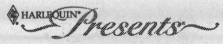

HARLEQUIN Presents

Seduction and passion guaranteed!

HARLEQUIN®
INTRIGUE

WE'LL LEAVE YOU BREATHLESS!

If you've been looking for thrilling tales of contemporary passion and sensuous love stories with taut, edge-of-the-seat suspense—then you'll love Harlequin Intrigue!

Every month, you'll meet four new heroes who are guaranteed to make your spine tingle and your pulse pound. With them you'll enter into the exciting world of Harlequin Intrigue— where your life is on the line and so is your heart!

THAT'S INTRIGUE—
ROMANTIC SUSPENSE
AT ITS BEST!

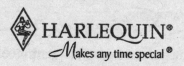

HARLEQUIN®
Makes any time special®

Harlequin® Historical

From rugged lawmen and valiant knights to defiant heiresses and spirited frontierswomen, Harlequin Historicals will capture your imagination with their dramatic scope, passion and adventure.

Harlequin Historicals . . . they're too good to miss!

HHDIR1

HARLEQUIN®

Makes any time special ®

HDIR1